A Meeting of Wolves

A Viking Omegaverse novella

LYX ROBINSON

A MEETING OF WOLVES

A Viking Omegaverse novella

LYX ROBINSON

Copyright © 2024 by Lyx Robinson

All rights reserved. No part of this publication may be reproduced, stored or transmitted in any form or by any means, electronic, mechanical, photocopying, recording, scanning, or otherwise without written permission from the publisher. It is illegal to copy this book, post it to a website, or distribute it by any other means without permission.

Published & illustrated by Lyx Robinson
www.lyxrobinson.com

CONTENT WARNINGS

In this novella there are graphic depictions of violence, battles, explicit M/M content and strong language.

For the best reading experience, this novella should be read after Taming the Wolves (Viking Omegaverse #2).

GLOSSARY

In this series, the Old Norse language includes some modern Icelandic phrases (which is the closest modern language to Old Norse), for anything I didn't find in my Old Norse resources.

Old Norse
Amma - Grandmother
Pabbi - Daddy (from Icelandic)
Jomsviking - A mercenary working for foreign lords/kings
Longphort - A ship fortress
Lyfjaberg - Literal "healing mountain"
Níðhöggr - Mythological serpent
Völva - A female magic practitioner
Thrall - A slave
Varg - Wolf, the term they use for Alphas
Vyrgen - Plural of Varg
Vanirdottir - The term they use for Omegas
Vanirdøtur - Plural of Vanirdottir
Yggdrasil - Mythological world tree

Norse culture
Loki in the caves: Refers to the tale of Loki's punishment. After killing the much-beloved god Baldr, Loki is chained in a cave where he is tortured by way of a snake dripping poison on him. Earthquakes are said to be caused by his struggling.
Máni: male personification of the moon. Brother to Sól, female personification of the sun.
Odin's Hávamál: A collection of wise adages & codes of conduct attributed to Odin.
Vestfold: A region in southern Norway.

Quick Pronunciation Guide
Norse Þ - hard 'th' like in thing
Norse ð - soft 'th' like in father

Chapter 7

Ivar
Dublin, 860
Waning Moon of December
Aftermath of the Battle of Mide

My wound was bleeding again; I could feel it trickling down my side. I stood in the light of the monastery's small windows, leaning against the stone, staring inside.

The abbot was walking through the main chapel in his long dark robes, lighting candles. It always amused me, how he acted as humble as a thrall though he wore gold and had a wife and children waiting for him in the village of Dublin.

His monastery was a sprawling stone building, rather large for its type. With our recent warring against the last High King of Ireland, the abbot had erected extra wooden enclosures for the injured, and many more tents sprouted like mushrooms over the grassy grounds.

Darkness lay over the holy place, stars blinking overhead. Even from where I stood, I could hear the groans of the injured, the industrious shuffling of monks and healers as they marched across the grounds.

There was no respite for them in the aftermath of war.

Half-dead with exhaustion and the clench of anger in my guts, I pulled my way around the monastery's stone walls until I came to the doors.

It took a moment for Abbot O'Fearghail to come. He slid back a small square panel to squint out into the darkness.

"Who goes there?" he called in his musical Gaelic. "It's late."

"*Deus auxilium, Pater,*" I hissed in the Latin he relished so. *God bless you, Father.*

The abbot drew in a breath upon hearing my voice. He had already recognised who stood at his door. A man can sense a wolf without seeing it. The hair bristles at the back of his neck; blood rushes up his spine; sweat beads upon his body.

I could smell him through the door. His fear and delight combined.

The door opened with a creak of hinges. He admitted me into his monastery, and I marched in, trying not to show that I had reopened my injury. He bowed his head in greeting.

"My lord Ivar Gofraidsson," he said as he shut and locked the door after me. He wore an amused little smile. "Your Latin is getting frightfully fluent."

"I have a good teacher," I told him, meeting his eye.

He was a tall, well-built man, wearing proof of a difficult rural life in his wide shoulders and hardened body. Though he wore his years in his greying beard and lined face, there was some grandeur about him that caught the eye, as though he were a king hiding in the simple robes of an abbot.

The last time I had paid him a nocturnal visit, it had been a full moon.

The silence was growing heavy as those memories lingered between us. Then he gave me a curt, respectful nod, as though to dispel the notion that I might have come for informal purposes when the moon was not high.

"Are you here to see your men?" he asked. "We have not lost any more since this morning."

"Good," I said. "I'd like to see them, yes. Lead the way."

He gestured for me to fall into step beside him, eyes raking down my body. I let him indulge himself, though he did not step too close nor linger too long. He seemed accustomed to satisfying himself with impressions alone, a quiet glimpse from a distance.

As the man should. He had a reputation to uphold, and any sexual kinship with a Viking would spread across it like tar.

The injured were a motley collection of Irishmen and Norsemen alike. They were the Dublin warband; all had fought under Olaf and I. The mingling of incense and herbal smoke stung my nose as we walked among the many sickbeds and tents.

I drifted between Gaelic and Norse, grasped sweaty hands and asked after the health of my raggedy pack. O'Fearghail would step closer to confirm whether they would soon get back on their feet. The Vyrgen were well on the way to recovery; the human men, less so.

Many of the Norsemen were not happy to be given sanctuary in a Christian monastery. And many of the monks were not happy to house pagans here, either. Our healers had been summoned to work side by side with them, but the collaboration was wrought with mistrust. Mostly they brushed shoulders as they kept to their own flock and ignored one another.

I sat with one of my best warriors, old Sigbrand, who

coughed and wheezed through his punctured abdomen.

"I should be in my own bed, Jarl," he rasped out. "We aren't welcome on this Christian soil. Their god looks unkindly upon me, I can feel him – sitting on my chest."

"It isn't their god but a spear wound, you idiot," I told him, tucking his covers away so I could see his bandages.

"He makes it fester," Sigbrand insisted. "He does not want us here."

"Do you see any Christian god above you?" I told him. "It is Máni that watches over you all. The darkness is his domain – the Christian god sleeps at this hour."

"Hrmph," he grunted. "He had better. I don't want to die under their wooden cross."

"Quit your moaning. Nothing can kill you, old man, we've already ascertained that."

He coughed out a laugh. I grasped his hand and was glad to feel him grasp me back firmly.

The Dublin warband had never been as large as this. The main reason we had shuttled this group into the monastery was that our own healers could not see to everyone. It was more pragmatic this way. The place was rich in resources – O'Fearghail had a hoard of medicinal plants and powders and instruments. It would be foolish not to work together.

Dublin was built on tangled languages and ancestries; it was the way of our pack to seek compromise and collaboration.

"She arrives tomorrow, doesn't she?" Sigbrand asked. "Olaf's bride. Isn't it tomorrow?"

His neighbours lifted their heads, and the question was on everyone's lips. "Is that right? She's arriving so soon?"

Anger clenched my gut again as I turned to face the speakers. "It is tomorrow, yes," I agreed.

"How is Olaf spending his last night as a celibate man?" Sigbrand asked. "Celebrating, I expect?"

"I'd say right now he's puking his guts out from stress," I told them, and they laughed. Many asked me to give Olaf and his bride their respects; others still requested that she might come here so they could get a look at her. I made what promises I could, then followed O'Fearghail back into the privacy of the stone corridors.

Ahead lay the door to his quarters, where he kept most of his medicinal stock under lock and key. It still felt strange, even after all these years, that we may work so closely together – we lords of Dublin and this monastery, which had preceded our entire settlement and had quietly watched us grow.

"Your monks are not happy," I said. He nodded wearily.

"They complain, but they would not turn away any injured man. We are all creatures of God."

I smirked at him. "Is that what you tell them?"

"They know it already."

"Speaking of creatures of god," I said as we approached the door, trying not to wince as my wound smarted. "I know your monks dislike coming down to the longphort. But the prisoners need care, and we're running short on supplies and healing hands. Do you have enough to spare?"

"Mm. I believe so."

O'Fearghail led the way into the abbot's quarters.

Cluttering the entrance were several large wooden trunks and one superb calligraphy easel. I traced the edge, not daring to touch the expensive parchment and inkwork he had stowed upon it. It fascinated me, the gold leaf he folded into the edges, the intricate knotwork he drew upon the margins.

All around the walls, endless shelves of apothecary equipment took up most of the space. The medicinal work was done upon a desk, in the light of the many lit candles that dripped wax on the wood. There was a pallet in one corner of the room, in case he needed to sleep here – of course, his real home was in Dublin.

I loved to come here. It was like squeezing through the roots of Yggdrasil and entering the lair of Mímir himself. O'Fearghail reached into his shelves and it was easy to see traces of the wise old god in him. Though doubtless he would disdain being compared to one of our gods.

We spoke of the state of certain prisoners, and he gestured to what he could spare, promising me that he would send monks down in the morning.

"Those prisoners," he said as he plucked a roll of linen bandages from a shelf. "How much longer are they staying?"

"They should be gone in the next few days."

Conversationally as ever, he asked, "Where are they headed?"

"Iceland has high demand at the moment."

He met my eye. We had already spoken of the holding of war prisoners in Dublin; he knew they were destined for long journeys and ports that needed free labour. As a Christian man, he disapproved of the very concept of slavery. But he lived alongside it, much like he lived alongside us *pagans*. He helped wherever he could, neutral bystander that he was.

"I thought your usual mode of functioning was to let their ports of harbour stitch them up instead of wasting your own resources on them," he said. "Could it be that you are learning to be selfless, my lord?"

I scoffed. "You know I am not a kind man, abbot."

"Ah. Of course. You want to heal them so they do not lose value."

Value. The word whispered across my shoulder blades, made me bristle.

"Correct, as ever," I said.

I waited for his usual chastisements, braced to rebuke them – I did not have the patience for philosophy tonight. But instead, he simply gestured for me to sit down on the bench, long sleeves gaping. I did so without thinking, letting out a quiet sigh of relief as my body relaxed some of its tensions.

"Let me see it," the abbot said.

I cocked an eyebrow at him. "See what?"

"Your injury."

Relieved of having to pretend, my hand came to grip my side. "It's fine," I muttered.

"It's bleeding through your tunic," O'Fearghail deadpanned. "How did your healers treat it?"

I imagined telling him of our ways, the Völva and her burning strands of wheat, offerings to the nine healing maidens. Her soot-blackened fingers dragging over me as she drew runes on my skin.

"I don't need your expertise," I grunted.

"The cursed do have the gift of fast healing," he said. "But it was a serious wound. Let me see."

He said it with the most serious, emotionless expression. I knew it well; it was a sturdy wall hiding many things, one I had already dismantled many a time only for him to cautiously build it up again.

I pulled off my belt and tunic.

O'Fearghail sat behind me. Just the heft of his body, the rustle of his robes, and already I was leaning back into his space, eyes heavy-lidded. I loved the scent of this room; it was the one he carried with him everywhere.

The dusty old parchment, the earthy black ink, the old smooth leather. The scent cradled me until my body pulsed with inappropriate associations.

His hands were steady as he unwound the bloody bandage and revealed the shallow axe wound that sliced into my waist. I hadn't even felt it – we had fought under the full moon, crazed as rabid dogs, savouring the scent of blood whether it was our own or our enemies'. But now the wound pulsed with pain, shortening my breath, making me giddy and hypersensitive.

"It's healthy," O'Fearghail said. "The stitches are well made."

"We savages do know a few tricks."

He scoffed at that, but chose to ignore it. "A normal man could not walk with this in his side," he said, his tone quiet and curious. "And yet you came up here to see your men regardless. You are more selfless than you think."

"I am not," I snapped. "I know you desperately want to believe I am redeemable somehow. You want to work alongside men who have some seed of goodness in them. But there is not a single redeemable quality within me, abbot."

"There is," he insisted. "Every man can be redeemed."

I tensed a little as he cleaned my wound. I was used to those hands on me in vastly different contexts. Perhaps that was why there was some strange, erotic quality to the way the abbot touched my side, his fingers slippery with blood.

Gently, he folded a compress over my wound. I hissed, leaning away – he held me firm, forced me to stillness with those large, sure hands. Though he sat behind me, I could feel his eyes roaming over my naked back. He had always been fascinated by my tattoos, the runes and fantastical creatures, the symbols of gods whom he had never spoken to.

The hand that steadied me slid down my side, dug a little into my skin. The familiar contact made me close my eyes.

"I did not come here to see my men," I admitted.

"Why, then?" he asked quietly.

He knew. He just wanted to hear me say it.

Pain pulsed through my body as he began wrapping linen around my waist. It was an ebb and flow of pain and growing delirium, my body filled with a strange, sticky sensation that made me want to laugh. He waited patiently for me to answer.

"I came here because..." How could I even put words to it? I could not even lay it down before any of the gods in a way that made sense. "Because there is something black and rotten in me," I muttered. "As you know. As you've seen. With the war, and now Olaf's bride... I feel I am shrinking while the rot spreads within me."

His words were softly spoken, contemplative: "What is this *rot*? How would you qualify it?"

I huffed. "I don't know. Selfishness, dishonesty perhaps. I'm not sure of the last time I was ever honest with anyone. There is a war within me between the man who seeks to be good, to be *functional,* and... the twisted creature that seeks to preserve itself."

"Are you being honest with me now?" the abbot asked. "Do you really seek goodness?"

"I think so," I said. "I hope so. I don't take pride in being this way – I just don't know how else to be."

"He who comes seeking God's counsel is already on the path to goodness."

I scoffed. "You know I only came to seek your counsel."

His hands hesitated in their bandaging, alighting on my waist.

The *counsel* I alluded to was not usually spiritual in nature. We only ever met at one another's fracture points; he was good at this type of talking, the *confessing*, as these Christians called it. But talking is not all we did.

He had black rot within him, too. And it could only be exorcised through word and deed.

He finished bandaging my waist, his arms embracing me with each layer he added. I let him, relishing his body heat as he drew closer. I needed him… needed him closer still. I wanted him to break me along those fracture lines, cutting clean edges so the pain might drain away.

I bared my neck for him.

He breathed in slowly as he recognised the honour I was paying him. He was a human man, but he knew exactly what such a signal meant from a Varg. He tied off the bandages, and then ran his fingers lightly over my neck, as though in awe that a Varg may offer him submission.

I wanted to hurt. These Christians and their delectation for blood and suffering – perhaps they were onto something. For right at that point, though I should've been drinking mead with Olaf in our great hall, I wanted instead for someone to twist and hurt me just like their Christ on the cross.

This was the highest point for Olaf and I. We had helped the High King of Ireland to win his crown, battering down his rival's armies in Mide. We were about to get a whole lot richer, in men and land and wealth. Our lives were poised at the pinnacle, teetering over the inevitable fall.

From here, we could only go down. Everything was going to change. Tomorrow, that woman's arrival would mark the beginning of a new life for us both. And I had no idea if we'd be able to go on as before, to chase the dreams we had always chased.

I wanted someone to push me over the edge, into the ravine, into the black.

"Do you have anything more you wish to confess," Abbot O'Fearghail murmured, "my son?"

I grinned as a twist of depraved delight clenched within me, making my cock throb.

"Do you, Father?" I whispered back.

He caught my long crested braid between his fingers, fisting my hair so that my spine bristled up. There was always some disdain in the beginning, as though he were accusing me of dragging him down into this filth. But his dispassionate pretence always devolved into hunger, nails biting into me, the reverence of a holy man giving in at last to what he desires most.

He did not kiss me. Some things he kept for his wife. Instead he bit into my flesh, holding me firm by the hair, and I closed my eyes to savour it.

It was usually the other way around. When I came here under the full moon, he would place himself beneath me, head bowed, pride bristling in the taut muscles of his shoulders, the bracing of his knees against the mattress. And he relished the pain of penetration, bore the brunt of my rut until it bloomed into pleasure. Oftentimes, tears ran down his cheeks to glitter in his beard.

That was the usual dynamic. My Varg instincts would not allow a human man to dominate me. But sometimes…

Sometimes the roles were reversed.

Submitting was not natural for either of us. For him, he had to swallow his ingrained pride, his Christian teachings that it was a woman's role to take. For me, it was the instincts of the Varg, roaring that to submit was weakness, that it made me dangerously vulnerable. Surely no one could be trustworthy enough to hold me down, lean over my back, breath on my neck.

But tonight, that danger was precisely what I needed. Bloody handprints stained my skin where O'Fearghail had grasped me, pulled aside my clothes, moved me carefully. I was gripping the edges of the bench – he loomed behind me, his mouth hovering over the back of my neck, hot breath prickling my skin.

With one hand he gripped my hip; with the other he parted my flesh. A slick slide of saliva to ease his passage, and he sank into me.

Pain, bright and blissful, crackled through me like lightning. My knees rocked against the hard wood of the bench, my nails biting into the edge as the solemn Benedictine gave in to the temptation I posed, the young feral pagan with everything to learn.

I could be many things for him. Usually I was Fenrir, the wolf that devoured.

Now I was the pup he delighted in educating. And he, the benevolent master.

The pain was everything. It filled me in a way that pleasure could not. Where pleasure would soothe like a warm bath, pain was electric, demanding attention, obliterating all thought until it was all that registered. It clanged against the sides of my skull, burned up my bones, glowed under my skin. To fight the animal instinct of curling into myself, and instead stretch out to let it fill me – yes, *yes,* the Christians were right to sacralise this.

Repentance. Retribution upon the flesh itself.

As Odin hung himself upon Yggdrasil, naked and bleeding, so I turned to my own gallows.

O'Fearghail had told me about their Christian idea of ecstasy. Something that overwhelms, that transcends the physical. This pain was like that – so strong that surely it would transform me to better express itself. There was some deep philosophy to learn in its throes; why we might push ourselves past our bodies' boundaries, why we might yearn to dance so close to death.

When O'Fearghail came at last, he clutched me to his chest, quiet breaths hot against my ear. As a Varg, I easily had the strength to overpower him. But I was here for this, that possessive grip of his, the neediness of it. I leaned back against him, panting as the ecstasy waned to a hot throb. The trickle of his seed stung as it dribbled down my thigh.

Still he held me by the black crest of my hair, the long braid twisted in his grasp. If his god were watching, surely he would see a human man grappling with a lean, hungry wolf.

"Again?" asked the holy man.

I felt close to blacking out. He was deep inside me, the shape of him searing me, though I was growing accustomed enough for the pain to ebb. He gave another thrust, slow and tender this time, and pleasure soothed up my spine in a tantalising promise.

"Yes," I hissed.

Chapter 2

IT WAS early morning by the time I made it back to Dublin's great hall, limping but sated. The hearthlight burned low, and a pleasant scent of dinner still filled the wide open space.

I stared at the doors beyond the long central hearth. They led to the royal quarters, where Olaf slept. Soon, he would welcome his own small family in those quarters.

I should've been glad for him. Olaf, my brother, always so put-together. He would make a good husband and a good father, we all knew it. He deserved this. But all I could feel was bitterness.

The Dubliners who had drank with Olaf last night were lumped in the benches and furs around the central hearth, snoring away. Deciding against the loneliness of my own quarters, I slumped among them, wincing from my fresh aches, and tried to sleep.

A Meeting of Wolves

ᛁ ᚠᚾᚱᚱ

It barely felt like any time had passed before morning light filled the hall and the thralls set to sweeping around us. Blinking my way out of the blank stupor I had sunk into, I realised suddenly that we would be expected to look presentable today. We were barely back from Mide; we had all turned to unkempt dogs over the past few months. None of us were even remotely ready for a wedding.

I reached for one of the larger axes and squinted into the gleaming metal. A tired, pale face stared back at me. My chin was darkened by the beginnings of a beard, which I never usually allowed. My crest of black hair was mussed from O'Fearghail's treatment of it. On either side of my head, bristly hairs had grown back, obscuring the tattoos I usually boasted.

Gods, O'Fearghail had seen me like *this* — it was a wonder he had accepted to touch me at all. I sat up properly, found a knife and set to shaving both sides of my head first. The beard would be next.

All around the hall, our stacks of armour and freshly cleaned weapons glinted in the dying firelight. It would all have to make way for flowers and the bridal gifts with which we'd welcome the Irish princess today. I could only savour the quiet while it lasted; the morning was going to bring with it a flurry of chaos.

The children were its first agents, naturally. I could hear them beyond the walls, cavorting in the streets of Dublin, having dragged their mothers out at the crack of dawn. Now that we'd brought all their fathers back from Mide, the little goblins were always underfoot.

I had barely finished shaving one side of my head before they burst into the hall, breaking the peace of early morning. Their mothers drifted in after them, tiredly greeting the thralls.

"*Oof!*" Armod burst awake as his son leapt onto his lap. "What—"

"It's morning, Pabbi!" the boy shouted. "Are you awake yet? Are you awake?"

Others grumbled and groaned. "Which one of Odin's balls did that one spring out of—"

"We're helping with the flowers," the boy went on, undeterred as his father straightened with difficulty. "We went to pick them at dawn with Amma. Do you want to see? Come and see."

The men stirred, grinning as they reached for their children, eyeing their wives from across the hall. Everyone was arriving with flowers and gifts for the coming bride. Everyone was excited to meet her.

Everyone it seemed, but me.

"Would you calm *down!*" I called at the children, holding my axe out of their reach, looking for any other wayward weapon they might hurtle against. They shrieked in their chaotic amusement, circling us like storms wearing human flesh. "What have I told you, you little rats! *No running in the hall!*"

The men only laughed at my feeble attempt to tame their unruly sons. Most of them let themselves be dragged away to be reunited with their tired, smiling wives. After the children had all ascertained that we were well awake, they left us at last. But not without first stomping on Orm, who was still managing to sleep somehow in the rising ruckus.

"What in Freya's name," he muttered hoarsely, nursing his stomped stomach. "Ivar? Why are there small children running everywhere?"

"Everyone's gathering to set up the bridal gifts," I said.

"So of course we've turned into a nursery for half of Dublin."

"Oh gods, is it morning already?" he groaned. "Here, pass me that axe."

I ran a hand over my freshly shaved skull before handing it over. The tattoos were stark and visible again, almost bluish in the morning light.

"Where were you last night, anyway?" Armod called to me as he got to his feet. "We had to coddle Olaf until past midnight."

"Yeah," chortled Orm. "Poor man was terrified. Could've used your company."

"He already had splendid company," I told them stiffly. "I'm sure you were more than adequate."

Then a deep voice filled the hall, making me freeze.

"There you are."

I turned, finding Olaf at the doors to the royal quarters. The great silver bear was frowning over the heads of several women, staring my way.

He seemed confused. Like he hadn't thought I would really desert him at such a crucial moment in his life. He was seeing me now in a new light, and he was clearly hurt.

I gritted my teeth. *This was his choice,* I reminded myself. *This breach between us is his fault.*

"Come on," he called to me, jerking his head toward his quarters. "I need you in here."

"Lifa and Ranog can help you," I called back, gesturing at the women who stood nearby him. "I have to fix my own face."

"Oh, just get in here, would you?" he snapped. "Thank you, ladies... I'll be fine, thank you."

He disappeared beyond the doors. I contemplated for a moment just getting up and leaving. That he would pretend any kind of unity still existed between us made me want to break things. But to prolong the rebellion would border on childishness, and I didn't want him to think I was simply being petulant.

It was serious, this time, the injury he had dealt.

With a sigh I straightened and followed him into his quarters.

ᛁᚠᚾᛦᛦ

Olaf was sitting straight as a pike in front of his large silver mirror. He was stony and stoic as ever, trying to appear calm though I could see sweat beading on his forehead. Dark rings under his eyes showed me he had not slept much, either.

I stood behind him with my hands in his long white-blond hair, twisting thin braids together, looping silver rings between the coils. It was an unconventional habit; the role would've been better suited to a sister, if we'd had one. Doubtless we did, somewhere out there in the wilderness, knowing our father. But I was the only bastard to have barged into the proud king's court; I was the only one to have been legitimised, once it became apparent that I would not simply vanish like a bout of spring rain.

Olaf had been glad to recognise me as his brother. He had always wanted one, lonely child that he was. Whether our father had been glad at all to acknowledge my existence was something far more debatable.

We were both silent and contemplative for a while, Olaf absently combing his ample beard with his fingers. Many things were coming to a close in this simple moment, this morning with its clear limpid light, its waiting and worrying and weaving tokens of stature into the hair of the husband-to-be.

A Meeting of Wolves

"You look sombre as Loki in the caves," Olaf muttered at one point. Startled out of my thoughts, I realised he was looking at me in the mirror.

It was a blatant opening. I swallowed, trying and failing to find a credible way to word my accusations.

I decided to play for time: "I'm just wondering."

"About what?"

I pulled back his hair. "Whether it wouldn't be better to just shave this all off," I said. "Look at that widow's peak. You aren't twenty any more, Olaf, you'll have to go egg-headed at some point—"

"Don't you *dare*," he said with a grin. "You haven't been able to persuade me for as long as I've known you, and you won't persuade me now."

I scoffed. Olaf had always had this idealised vision of himself as a successful man; he would be a great hairy Jarl just like his father, with his own hall and a rich legacy to leave his children. The long hair was non-negotiable. It marked him, made him recognisable as the Jarl of Dublin, son of King Gofraid, a silver-haired prince among men.

But it had deeper meanings, too. He kept his hair long because he had other, private dreams. A woman would thread her fingers through it; a child would tug on the braided lengths. It was a commitment to those goals, the life he had always strived towards.

Until now, we had both always assumed that a Vanirdottir would step into the role one day. Olaf's wife would naturally be a princess of legend, a woman of high enough status to stand by his side. She had been an idea, an elf dancing on the edge of our world, a giddy dream that led us both on.

But now, after all these years of searching far and wide for those legendary womenfolk… he was settling for a human woman after all.

Cutting short the chase. Curtailing our dream.

"I know why you're sulking," Olaf said. His shrewd grey eyes were still fixed on me in the mirror. I glared at him.

"I do not *sulk*."

"Yes you do." His eyes narrowed. "You think I'm giving up."

I held his gaze, teeth gritted firm. "Well, aren't you?"

"No," he said. "Of course not. Everything will go on as usual, little brother. We will go on hunting the Vanirdøtur as we always have."

"Everything will not go on *as usual*," I said. "You'll be married. You'll be a father, eventually. And this allegiance to the High King of Ireland means you've committed to fight his battles for years to come. You won't have the time to chase dreams."

"Of course I will. I'll make the time," Olaf countered. "But it is as you say, Ivar: the Vanirdøtur are a dream. I don't want to spend all my time reaching out into the darkness for something elusive. I want to live a semblance of a life, and you should, too."

I raised my eyebrows at him in the mirror. I didn't know how to express the explosion of disdain his words provoked in me.

The Vanirdøtur were a dream, yes. We had chased magic all our lives, yearning for a glimpse of the elves, or the chance to catch Níðhöggr by the tail. Then as we grew older, we committed to finding Freya's daughters, bloody palms clasped in a promise.

It was an infamous hunt that many men had attempted. Throughout history, those men had left enough cryptic clues in their wake to kindle our fervour. We decided that we would be the ones to find them and draw them back into the world. That was what would make our reputation; our names would live on as those two brothers who found Freya's daughters at last.

We had committed together. But Olaf was the eldest. He had always been the one leading the way. And now, with how he had decided to abruptly upend both of our lives, I realised just how much control he had always had over the accomplishment of our dream.

More and more, it felt like I had been merely following in his footsteps. I was the younger brother, the bastard who would amount to naught if it weren't for him, pulling me after him. If he was no longer committed, could I accomplish it alone? Would anyone follow me if I did not have Olaf by my side?

I knew the answer, and it rankled me more than I cared to admit.

"You already have far more than a *semblance of a life*," I snapped at him. "You say that as if you had not built Dublin with your own hands, pulled together a solid warband out of mercenaries and drifters, earned your glory on countless battlefields. You have a solid name already, Olaf. This is a good life."

His gaze softened. "This is a good foundation," he said quietly. "But you know there is more to life than names and dreams alone."

"You only say that because you *have* a name," I said. "You could choose to do anything you like. Follow this dream or that one. You have men aplenty, and I—"

I trailed off before I could sound even more pathetic and envious. Olaf's expression was kind and understanding, and that grated all the more.

"I built my name," he said. "I built this place because it was necessary, to have a foothold away from Father. To rally men to our cause, to have somewhere we could call our own. You – you are a dreamer, Ivar. If you were the one leading us, we would be sleeping under bushes, earning our pittance with songs, trying to find the Vanirdøtur by peering through the branches."

I could only laugh, surprised by his bluntness. "Well, fuck you."

"It's true, brother," he said. "You don't have a pragmatic mind. You have all these fantastic ideas but you hardly dare to make them concrete reality. If we're to reach for the elusive, we must have our feet firmly planted on the ground."

I finished his hair, combed it back over his head so it would flow elegantly down past his shoulder blades. He said it as though I were content to drift and dream. But in reality… I wanted nothing more than to be more like him, pragmatic, focused. Successful. If he wanted a kingdom, a legacy, a wife and children – he simply reached out and took them.

Why could I not do the same? Somehow I could not bring myself to expect those things, to feel entitled to them. I could not really imagine ever obtaining what I most wanted.

Olaf ran a hand down his braided hair, gazing at it approvingly in the mirror. Then those shrewd eyes met mine again. "We will find the Vanirdøtur," he assured me, his tone firm. "You say I have committed to fighting the High King's battles. I have indeed. But those battles will lead us across all of Ireland, brother. If there are any clues in this country, we will be well placed to find them."

Those words warmed me a little. But there was still one uncomfortable detail which I did not know how to bring up kindly.

There was no other way to put it:

"What will your human wife think, if we do bring home the Vanirdøtur one day?"

He got up with a sigh, as though he had been expecting that very question all this time. Then he turned around to face me, placing both hands on my shoulders, his face genial as ever.

"Well, I expect my wife will brew honey-milk for them, and lay out bread and stew on the table so we may eat our fill after the long journey," he said. "And we will throw many feasts for all those men who will take a Vanirdottir's hand in marriage."

I cocked an eyebrow at him. "You will not envy them the prize?"

"No, Ivar," he said. "I have made my choice. I would rather live now than wait for some ephemeral image of perfection to darken my door. I'm not getting any younger, as you said. I'm tired of coming home to an empty room."

I sighed and nodded. He was like this; blunt and decisive. He would not go back on this decision. I knew him well enough to be sure of that.

He pulled me into an embrace, patted me on the back. I frowned into his shoulder, feeling foolish and shameful for having left him last night to sink into my usual chaos.

"We will carry on the chase, little brother," Olaf said. "It may take more time, and we may take longer pauses. But I know you'll understand eventually. Once you get to my age, you'll see."

I scoffed. Ever since reaching thirty, he had become an endless well of old men's adages. "You barely have three hairs on your chin and already you speak like an ancient."

He chuckled as he pulled away, scrubbing his knuckles over the thick white-blond beard that was far denser than what I suggested. "Well, I'm getting there."

"I just never thought you'd settle for a human woman," I muttered.

"Oy." He scowled at me, his amusement waning. "That's my wife you're talking about. You will not use those terms for her."

A pang echoed through me. Already she was affecting him, wedging herself between the two of us, and she had not even arrived in Dublin.

No. He was right. I was being pathetic, bitter towards a woman I had not even met yet. And I could very well use the same terms for myself – Olaf had settled for what was available with me, too. A half-brother dragged out of the Völvas' caverns, scruffy and unkempt, but alive.

He deserved better than me. He deserved everything. But somehow he was content to enjoy what was available to him; and I kept on doubting that such a thing was possible.

When Olaf and I found ourselves in these moments, these liminal spaces between one life and the next, I regressed. I turned back into that scruffy-haired boy, the one who held onto what scant little he had until his own fingers bled. I had to be better.

I let go of my older brother and stepped away from him.

"Come on then," I told him. "You're as ready as you'll ever be. Let's go."

Chapter 3

"THE PRINCESS *comes! Vírún of Clann Uí Néill comes!*"

The cry preceded a great cacophony of hooves clattering into Dublin. Olaf and I stood in the courtyard of the great hall as the procession approached. Villagers had gathered from all over town and the environing farmsteads to welcome Olaf's betrothed at last.

I lifted my chin, squinting to ward off the morning sunlight. In one hand I held my bronze pendant depicting Freya, large as an apricot seed, the cord twisted around my wrist. I turned and turned the statuette in my fingers. Since I was a child, the familiar shape of her would soothe my baser impulses. But even she could not soothe the clench of anger in me now.

Olaf stood tall and proud beside me in his furs, groomed to perfection. He smiled at me, and I could see the sparks of nervous anticipation in him, though he worked to appear calm as ever.

I forced a smile. I wish I could've reciprocated sincerely. Enjoyed the moment more fully with him.

But I couldn't.

It was hard to see the bride properly. Hooded and cloaked, she rode ahead of a long trail of riders and horse-drawn carts, presumably her ladies and belongings. Flanking her were six stony-faced guards. They were Norsemen bearing the patterned shields of mercenaries, the Irish High King's hired Jomsvikings.

I squinted harder as one of them drew my eye.

He rode nearest to the princess. A young man with tousled golden hair, far younger than all the rest. He was strikingly handsome, if one could look past the sullen expression and the scar that marred his face.

I tilted my head to the side, muttering to myself: "Who is that splendid creature riding into our courtyard?"

Olaf raised his eyebrows. "You're talking about my bride?"

"I meant the man beside her."

He scoffed. "Of course."

"Isn't he young for a Jomsviking? And his face. He looks like Baldr himself."

"Baldr on a bad day, then."

He wasn't wrong. The other Jomsvikings weren't exactly wearing big toothy smiles, but the look on that boy's face could've curdled milk. Baldr, the most beautiful of Odin's golden-haired sons, had clearly stepped in shit this morning.

The procession came to a halt, the Jomsvikings spacing out to dismount before the princess. I watched as the young Baldr swung gracefully down from his horse.

Then he turned, and I saw his scar in full. And I understood better why he looked so sour.

It wasn't a scar. It was an X-shaped cattle brand.

Old fears shivered up my spine. I remembered vividly the sound of sizzling iron in the fire, the smell of burnt flesh. The fear of that brand being placed on me.

It was the brand of the exiles of Vestfold. It made one untouchable, back in the kingdoms of Norway. Any branded Norseman who would arrive in Ireland seeking a new life would not be welcomed by their Norse kin. And the Irish had caught on to the notion, so that even freedmen could not rise above the status of untouchable.

And yet this branded exile stood close to the princess as though there were kinship between them.

"My lords Olaf and Ivar Gofraidsson," intoned one of the older Jomsvikings, bowing to us. "Please welcome our dearest Princess Vírún to your hall. His Grace Aed Finliath, patriarch of Clann Uí Néill and High King of Ireland, extends his warmest regards, and promises to arrive in time for the wedding..."

Vírún pulled down her hood. All at once, everyone's attention shifted from the branded Jomsviking to the princess herself.

She was... plain. Her face was square and unfeminine, dark eyes looking down a hawk nose as they searched for Olaf's. Her skin was pockmarked with spots and acne scars, her hair black and twisted into a thin braid. She was older too than the youthful image we had all doubtless crafted in our minds. Gold gleamed on her ears and around her neck, but otherwise, there was nothing about her that alluded to her status as an Irish princess of ancient lineage.

She dropped into a curtsey. Silence reigned. For a moment I wondered if all those in our courtyard were thinking the same thing, that surely such a strange looking woman would not be acceptable for our Jarl. Olaf was well-loved by all in Dublin, and many gravitated to him at our full moon feasts. He tended to be exclusive with those partners he chose, and many had already sought to tempt him into marriage. I could almost hear their thoughts now – *Olaf safeguarded himself all those years for this? For her?*

Vírún quaked as the silence went on. Though I judged her just as harshly as the rest at first, I saw then the tremor in her hand. The way she dropped her head, as though embarrassed to show her face.

She and her branded Jomsviking made an odd pair indeed. Of course, Vírún did not need to be beautiful for the populace of Dublin to cheer; she wore enough gold to impress them. One set the cry, and the others soon followed, cheering in welcome. They came closer to shower her with petals, which caught in her hair and on the capes of her Jomsviking guards. I tore my eyes away from the sight of the young Baldr with blood-red petals in his hair, and looked at my brother.

Olaf gazed at his bride for the first time, holding himself still and emotionless as a rock. He wore his silver wolf furs as a sign of his stature; what with his jewelled hair and polished leathers, he had preened himself to resemble a Varg prince from a saga. And Vírún appeared all the more painfully human in contrast.

I wondered what he thought of her.

Could he really be content with this? Vírún was a contract. She was here to seal our alliance with Aed Finliath, the freshly crowned High King of Ireland. She and Olaf had never even met before, and I doubted she was Olaf's type, judging from the partners he chose under the full moon. She was a purely pragmatic choice. Olaf deserved the world, and he was settling for *good enough*.

Vírún's eyes crossed mine, and she dipped her head almost immediately. Her hands shook as she gripped her skirts. With a pang I wondered if my expression told her what I thought of her.

Human, uninteresting, another commonplace Irish princess. Who do you think you are, to deserve my brother? To turn his head from our quest?

The young Baldr stepped closer to her and, to my astonishment, *glared* straight at me.

I stumbled in my bitterness just for a moment. Of course Vírún had had no choice in this; I had no right to be unkind to her. But the insult of the young Baldr's challenge rankled.

I stared him down icily. He should know better than to challenge a mature Varg on his own territory.

Olaf stepped forward, breaking all tensions. He gave his bride a warm, reassuring smile as he closed the distance between them. The contrast between her plain appearance and his large glittering fur-clad frame was almost absurd. But he took her hand, as though to challenge any who would see issue in their joining – and he kissed her knuckles without further ado.

"Princess Vírún of Clann Uí Néill," he intoned. "Welcome to Dublin."

The crowds cheered again. Vírún's pock-marked face cracked into a smile, and suddenly I saw her, the woman that she was rather than the contract dressed in gold. Even the young Baldr's sullen face softened a little as the villagers showered the couple with petals a second time.

She was going to be my sister-in-law.

So this was it. The first step in the new life Olaf had chosen for us. He had made the decisions, turned us both into this new direction, as he always had. I stared at his broad back, unable to shake the feeling that he was letting our old life fly away from his hands, and that there was nothing I could do to snatch it back.

I avoided looking at Vírún as we led her into the great hall, and I had a feeling she avoided me just the same.

ᛁ ᚠᛁᚱᚱ

We threw a feast for her, inviting all those karls who could fit into our great hall. Olaf and I sat as ever in the place of honour, facing the whole hall. Behind us bloomed our altar to Freya; the pillar carved in her likeness, the fresh flowers and feather arrangements, the short swords stuck into the beaten earth floor at her feet. Except this time Vírún sat with us, wedged between us, her back to the goddess.

It made me bristle when neither Vírún nor Olaf offered the goddess any sign of respect. Freya had watched over us as we fought to earn her favour, to prove our worth and earn the right to find her daughters. And now a human woman sat here in the place where Freya's daughter should've sat; and we were forsaking the goddess who had guided us all these years. She who had won us many gruesome battles, who had seen that Dublin's fields grow plentiful, and who had been as a mother to us as we navigated strange lands.

She stood silent behind us now like the old greying matron who, disappointed but not surprised, accepts to be forgotten.

Vírún's Jomsvikings hovered around the room, wary at first, then finally relaxing and joining in the chatter and laughter. The young Baldr, however, did not. He stood by the doors of the great hall like a solitary guard hound, watching us, a hand on his axe hilt. No doubt his cattle brand warded his fellows away from casual kinship. Or perhaps he simply didn't like company.

Though he was an upstart little pup, I felt some

kinship with him. I was hardly in the mood for feasting and laughter, either.

The chatter was good-natured, mainly aiming at mocking Olaf for being celibate for so long. The men teased Vírún, saying she was a blessing who would restore his youth to him. She smiled, but she was no young maiden who might blush and stammer about these things. Being close in age to Olaf, there was maturity and elegance in her manner.

We all saw it, as the meal progressed. They were well-suited. They both knew why they had come together, and they both accepted it with a kind of grace I had not anticipated. There was no awkwardness; they both fell into an easy dynamic, as though they were long-standing allies who understood their roles in this collaboration. He touched her hand several times over the meal, and she did not protest it; she only looked at him and smiled quietly as though she had expected such things.

Well, of course she would not protest his attentions. Olaf was a handsome, intelligent man. She must be very happy indeed with her catch.

I forced myself to glare down at my stew instead of my brother. He was happy, too... he was content with his choice.

Gods, why couldn't I just be happy for him?

"My father mentioned something about you," Vírún said once she had warmed enough to the men to lead the conversation. "I thought I'd ask, now that I'm here... he said you men of Dublin chase myths throughout the kingdoms of Ireland."

Olaf bristled almost imperceptibly beside her. I fought the urge to smirk. Her restating our abandoned quest herself was the finest irony. She was here, after all, to slip fine fur slippers upon Olaf's cold feet.

I spoke up for the first time: "Indeed, that *was* our primary reason for coming here."

Olaf's glare was like a hammer striking an anvil. "We came here chasing a rumour," Olaf said, hoping to drown me out. "It's said that the children of old gods reside in your forests."

Children of old gods, he said. A carefully neutral way to refer to the Vanirdøtur.

"That's interesting," Vírún said, tilting her head. "Do you mean the *aes sidhe?*"

A murmur went around the table as those with Irish wives nodded and those who did not know the term looked perplexed.

"That is one lead we have been following," Olaf said with a nod.

"Who are the *aes sidhe?*" one of the karls asked.

"The Fair Folk," Vírún said. "They're said to reside all around us, beneath the ground, in groves and forests."

"My wife says the Fair Folk are descendants of your gods," another karl mentioned. "The Tuatha dé Danann."

"Your pronunciation is very good," Vírún said with a smile. "That is the story you hear from old farmers. But the Tuatha dé Danann are not divine in their own right. They are creatures of the one God, angels who fell to the earth a long time ago."

"In any case," Olaf said, lifting his chin. "Chasing myths is not currently a priority. We have enough on our plate, if we're to help your father reclaim his rightful territories one by one."

"Oh, really?" Vírún swivelled around to Olaf, head still tilted. "That's a shame. I've read many things about the *aes sidhe*; I've chased them a little myself. I think it makes for a good reprieve from war, to chase magic instead. My father will drag you across all of Ireland to take back his lands; you'll be at liberty to look all over."

Both Olaf and I stared at her in surprise.

Oh, if she only knew of whom she spoke. I wonder if she would show herself to be so enthusiastic then.

"Perhaps," Olaf conceded. Then he cleared his throat, turned the conversation fully to war, and left behind what he now considered fancies.

I slumped again as everyone spoke of our recent victory in Mide, the first of many battles we would fight in Aed Finliath's name. Olaf seemed relieved. There was no longer any need to glare at me, so he ignored my existence altogether.

Good. I could not abide staring into his irritatingly jovial face one second longer.

The men spoke of Olaf's exploits on the battlefield, aggrandising them until he was laughing and holding up his hands to feign humility.

"You speak as though I ended the war single-handedly," Olaf protested. "I did not. We have Thrain Mordsson to thank for that."

"Aye!" Several karls lifted their goblets. "To Thrain!"

Others joined in until all the table was united in the toast, spilling mead droplets everywhere. "Thrain Mordsson, the kingslayer! The terror of Ireland!"

"Did you know him, princess?" one karl asked Vírún, leaning across the table. "Is it true he was one of your father's men?"

Vírún wore a curious smile. Her gaze crossed the hall to meet the young Baldr's, and something passed between them, that kinship I had glimpsed outside.

"You speak as though he were no longer among us," Vírún said.

"*Was* he ever among us?" Olaf asked. "Some say he was not just a simple Norseman but Thor disguised on the battlefield."

Vírún laughed. "I didn't know you men of Dublin had such stories about him."

"Surely your father's armies raise their cups in his name, up there in the Uí Néill," Olaf said. "It was a long, bloody war – if I ever met him, I would want to embrace him as a brother for putting an end to it all."

A shadow passed over Vírún's face, then. The glance she exchanged with her young branded Jomsviking was strained this time.

"My father's men should," she said slowly. "They should recognise him. He is a brave, capable young man. But they do not appreciate him as he just deserves."

The young Baldr bristled by the door, breaking off their gaze. The other Jomsvikings all stirred too; Vírún was including them in her accusation.

Curiosity bubbled in me to see the pup so discomfited. Clearly he had some insight into whatever secret Vírún was withholding.

"Why not?" asked Armod. "Why would they not celebrate him? The Irishmen of the Uí Néill are friends of the Vikings."

"Aye. You being here is but proof of it," nodded Orm, and many karls raised their goblets again.

"Thrain Mordsson wears the brand," Vírún said at last. "The brand of the exiles of Vestfold."

A silent spell rippled out from that fact. Many men around the table winced, glancing at one another. It was a shameful thing, a strike on one's honour. I could see a mixture of empathy and vague vestiges of fear around the table.

I was not the only one to glance across the hall at her branded Jomsviking. He had turned his face firmly away now, obscuring the brand from view.

Excitement leapt in my gut. Could he possibly be...?

No. Many wore the brand on the northern coasts of Ireland. And he was just a pup.

"Vestfold," Olaf said wonderingly. "Then Mord, his father... I do believe I knew him. He was one of the six chieftains that ruled there, back in our day."

Vírún looked surprised. "You know the place?"

"Vestfold is our homeland," Olaf told her. "Well, mine and my brother's, and all those old greybeards you see around the table. We know their practices intimately." Raising his voice in disdain, he added, "We all generally agree that those pretender-kings who wield the iron should receive thirty brands in the centre of their own faces."

Several of the old Dubliners raised their cups, shouting their approval. Olaf spoke louder over the growing noise:

"If my father had not escaped Norway in time, we would've worn the same brand. And he's now King of the Southern Isles!"

Many a cheer leapt up at that. "Aye," Sigbrand interjected. "What do the Irish know of Norse politics? The brand means nothing to them. There should be no ill will towards those who wear it."

Some debate arose regarding the different Norse settlements here in Ireland and surviving traditions there. But Vírún's eyes were fixed on her branded Jomsviking. My mouth parted as I watched them both move at the same time.

She rose to her feet; he pushed against the doors of the great hall, hoping to slip out unnoticed.

"Wait," Vírún called to him. "Thrain. Wait."

The silence that filled the hall now was absolute. All sound drained from the air, until all that was left was the wet munching of the dogs in the corners of the hall.

Everyone was staring at the young Jomsviking now. He was breathing hard, his chest heaving as he stayed stuck by the door, obeying his princess's order.

"Come, Thrain," Vírún called. "You're among friends."

He looked over his shoulder at her, frowning, and the betrayal in his face was almost painful to look upon.

"You mean to tell me," Olaf said, slowly pushing himself up to his feet beside her. "That I have the man himself in my hall? And nobody thought to say so before now?"

The pup looked once at Olaf and away again, as though burnt by my brother's resplendence.

"Boy," Olaf called to him directly, switching to Norse. "Are you truly the one we've been shouting about and toasting like fools?"

He did not answer.

It was him. It had to be him.

Elation gripped me as I watched the pup turn, eyes on the ground, frowning. Interestingly, though he quaked on the spot to have been found out, he did not turn his neck in submission.

"Step closer where I can see you," Olaf ordered. Thrain Mordsson – tracked now by everyone in the hall – marched across the beaten earth until the central hearthlight glowed upon his features.

The brand only accentuated his cheekbones and the elegant dips of his face. I stared, hardly able to believe who I was looking at. He was more notorious than Olaf and I – and yet he was barely out of adolescence.

Sensing the pup's discomfort, Olaf strode slowly to him and placed his hands on Thrain's shoulders.

"It's an honour to have you in my hall," Olaf said. "It is as the princess says. You are among friends here."

Finally, a hoarse voice croaked from Thrain's lips:

"Thank you, Jarl."

Olaf grinned, patting him on the shoulder. Then he grasped Thrain's wrist and lifted it into the air.

"Thrain Mordsson!" he intoned, and everyone set to cheering. Vírún looked upon her Jomsviking as though this had been something she had always hoped for him; wholehearted acceptance from a pack of his Norse kin. But from his face, you'd have thought we were throwing him in the gallows.

Chapter 4

By the next day, everybody in Dublin knew who had escorted Olaf's bride to our hall. Farmers who had nothing to do in their snowy fields lingered in town just for a glimpse of the famous Thrain Mordsson. But while they all hoped to speak with him and have him recount his infamous duel with the late High King, they were quickly disappointed. He kept to his task of protecting Vírún, staying stony-faced and prickly, and did not speak to anyone.

Vírún didn't need to be so closely protected once the courtship was properly begun. Olaf laughed over the pup's insistence to shadow their footsteps everywhere they went. He shook Thrain Mordsson off fondly, even going so far as to ask whether the pup was going to follow them into the bedchamber – and Thrain stepped away after that.

Olaf and Vírún discussed him one night, alone in

the great hall. I was returning from stabling the horses, and when I heard their quiet tones, I slowed and stalled behind a pillar. Not that I *wanted* to eavesdrop – they just didn't make it easy to give them privacy when they were always staying up late to talk.

Well. Maybe I was a little curious, too.

"... indeed, there were still six chieftains in Vestfold, back in our day," Olaf was saying. "But we don't hear much from the old country now, apart from when we meet fresh arrivals. We only know everything's changed in recent years."

Vírún nodded. "You know about the man who broke apart the rule of the six, then? The one who called himself king in Vestfold?"

"Harald Fairhair," Olaf said, the name little more than a growl.

"That is the name on Thrain's lips," Vírún said. "You say it like he does. I've never heard a name spoken with so much hatred."

"Harald Fairhair is the spawn of a rotten, power-hungry family," Olaf said grimly. "They are the reason Ivar and I spent most of our lives down here in the isles of Britannia rather than back home."

I stared up at the wall. Funny that he would call it home. But then, Olaf had seen more of Vestfold than me; what memories I had of the place were not particularly bright and happy.

It was actually quite endearing to hear Vírún try to understand the workings of Vestfold as an outsider. Clearly she had listened carefully to her servants' stories and committed them to memory, seeking to understand how the world of the Norsemen functioned.

"From what I hear, Harald Fairhair's ascension to power was bloody," she said. "He sought to break the six chieftains one by one so they would submit. Thrain's village was burned, and his father was killed in a public ceremony – something about an eagle, nobody would explain it to me…"

My blood ran cold. Thrain had witnessed his own father on his knees, ribs broken, lungs torn out to make the bloody wings of the eagle.

"… and naturally Thrain had to be broken, too. As the son of the chieftain, he could've become a standard around which the resistance would've gathered. His mother was very well-loved, too – Harald Fairhair would've taken her as a second wife if she had not resisted him. So Thrain and his mother were branded and thrown into the wilderness to fend for themselves…"

She paused, as though empathy had choked her words. There was a rustle of fabric, Olaf leaning closer to her for reassurance.

"Such are the tales of the branded," he muttered. "Broken lives, broken legacies."

"Thrain and his mother arrived on our shores when he was still a child," Vírún said. "And I thought our Norse settlers would be sympathetic to them, but they were not. They view the branded as little more than slaves. Thrain and his mother were caught up in the trade for a while, and his mother grew very weak. So Thrain broke them out of bondage and tried to find sustenance for them both. He was barely ten at the time, and he had to… well. Survive, I suppose."

A pause. I traced lines along the pillar absently, heart thudding as I imagined what a childhood it must've been. No wonder Thrain was wary of simply accepting our friendship. It would take a great deal to rebuild his trust in his own kin.

"He was a feral child," Vírún said. "He first came to

my father's attention because he'd killed a group of our Norse mercenaries. He was *ten* and he managed... I don't know how. I've never seen a boy fight like him. It's like he becomes possessed."

My mouth ran dry. Ten years old, and capable of taking on a whole group of Vyrgen mercenaries? I stared at the wall, curiosity raging.

Though the tale was fraught with tragedy, I knew I had to see this for myself. How Thrain Mordsson fought.

Olaf spoke up: "So instead of condemning him, your father chose to take him on as a mercenary?"

Vírún paused. "That was my father's intention," she said. "He saw Thrain's potential. But I saw a ten-year-old boy, and a woman stripped of all that made her who she was. I wanted to give them somewhere they could have enough peace to be restored to themselves. So they came to live with us. But..."

She sighed.

"It isn't easy. People see the brand and recoil. Thrain's mother manages to garner more sympathy as my lady-in-waiting, but Thrain himself... he is very solitary." There was another rustle of fabric. I glanced beyond the pillar and saw Vírún smiling up at my brother, leaning intimately close. "You are the first to welcome him with open arms. For that, I'm very grateful."

"Of course," he rumbled. I rested my eyes on them a moment, still thinking of Thrain's harrowing childhood. Olaf reached up to trace Vírún's jawline, and before I could look away, he leaned in and kissed her. I jerked around to face the wall as some strange, sickening feeling crackled through me.

Olaf was not one to display physical affections publicly. Seeing them both move around Dublin, you'd think theirs was a cool and pragmatic relationship. But I knew the courtship between a Varg and a human woman involved intimacy before the wedding itself. It was necessary to prepare her for the unique attributes of a Varg, which human women had difficulties taking.

From the enthusiasm of that kiss, it was obvious they'd already begun. They were just keeping it to themselves.

"Any friend of yours is my friend," Olaf told her in a murmur. "Wife."

"Thank you," she said, her voice low and private. "I would say the same to you… though I'm not sure your brother would want my friendship."

"My brother is an ass," Olaf said. I raised my eyebrows. *Nice.*

"He's a little… intimidating," Vírún admitted with a laugh. "I think he's been avoiding me."

"You frighten him, because you are made of flesh and not air," Olaf said. "He enjoys chasing dreams far more than he does building something real."

I blinked at the wall, chest hollow as though he had just sent forth a volley of arrows at me. He'd said as much to my face before – but to hear him say it to someone else in confidence was somehow worse in its condescension. They were like two parents, sighing over their problem children.

"That's harsh, isn't it?" Vírún said. "He's your brother."

For the first time I felt a little true warmth towards her. Harsh, indeed! I threw a feast for the damn man.

"I love him more than anything, of course," Olaf rumbled. "But he frustrates me. He has a brilliant mind, but he does not think himself capable of putting his ideas into motion. He wants to reach his impossible ideals and yet he does not build any kind of ladder to reach them. It's like he hopes the gods will teach him to fly."

I breathed out slowly, trying to quell the urge to get

up and drag him to the floor. Oh, I would make him eat his own words, and the hearth ash with them.

"Didn't you build Dublin together?" Vírún asked.

Olaf huffed with laughter. "It's more that I built a sturdy ladder, and he stands upon it with me and says, *the wood isn't good enough quality. The rope is frayed, look. You could do better.* Even while his hands stay white and soft enough to play the tagelharpa and weave songs while I work."

"Not everyone is a carpenter," Vírún said. "Without someone to point you in the right direction, perhaps your ladder would be crooked."

My heart thudded. She, of all people, was defending me.

The shock of their words began to melt into pooling heat, like blood seeping from a wound. I pushed away from the pillar and left them, seeing red.

So I had contributed nothing, had I? Olaf had built up this entire endeavour alone while I was content to sing fucking songs? Is that how he saw it?

Well then. If I was so useless to him, there was nothing stopping me from simply leaving and taking matters into my own hands. Let him present himself before the High King of Ireland like an overeager pup on his first full moon feast if that's what he really wanted.

Perhaps Thrain Mordsson had the right idea about remaining solitary. He had survived against towering obstacles, prevailed somehow, and now he was the talk of Ireland. His experiences had shaped him, made him capable of holding his own against all odds. Even at *ten years old*. When I was ten, I was still the bastard child hiding behind the brilliant young Prince Olaf, relishing his protection. And I had never stepped out from behind him.

If I stayed in my brother's shadow all my life, how could I ever make a name for myself as Thrain had?

How could I achieve anything?

I slipped my pendant over my head, tucking Freya into my tunic so she could take warmth from my skin. I would go and find the Vanirdotur alone. Leave Olaf to all of his grand accomplishments. If he did not need me… then I would make sure I no longer needed him.

Chapter 5

In the stables stood a great white stallion, radiating the calm strength of a giant. Alsvithr. He was Vírún's stallion; Olaf had picked him out for her as a wedding present. His white coat was doubtless a symbol of the peaceful alliance that united them.

I yanked the bit into his mouth. Right then I could not abide peace. Olaf was on his little cloud, huddling up with his wife-to-be, fantasising about the good grounded life that lay ahead of them both. He was content, and his simple contentment made me crave violence.

If I was not setting a torch to the great hall's thatched roof, it was only because of the love I bore my brother. But my fingers itched to spill fire, eyes drawn to the torches on the walls.

The white stallion bent to my commands as easily as anything. We trotted out through the main courtyard and along the snowy, beaten-earth roads of Dublin. The light seeping through sleepy farmhouse windows illuminated us, hearthfires kept kindled all through the night. The thick coating of snow on the fields and roofs was almost bluish in the darkness.

Not many would follow me if it meant leaving Dublin, leaving Olaf. But there were those Dubliners who were true disciples of Freya, like me. We had already met to discuss Olaf's change of heart multiple times. It would be enough to form a band to travel with, once the snows melted and spring brought with it the opportunity for adventure.

All I had to do was visit those faithful karls and tell them... tell them I had made my decision.

We would leave come the spring.

My hands trembled around the reins. The thought of leaving my brother... I had never ventured anywhere without him.

I clenched the reins tighter. It was just the winter cold making me shake.

I was not *afraid*. I could survive without Olaf. I could *thrive* without him. He had only ever held me back. Without him... I could prove my worth at last.

All heroes wandered alone.

"Come on... get a hold of him!"

There was rustling and shouting behind me. Whatever was happening scared a herd of black sheep – they scurried past me along the road, making Alsvithr snort and chuck up his head. I collected him and halted, one hand on my sword hilt, squinting behind myself at the commotion.

Men were regrouping on the main road, surrounding whoever it was they'd been chasing. I recognised about a dozen of Vírún's Jomsvikings, who'd clearly been at the mead tonight.

"Makes me sick," one of the large bearded men growled, stepping into the centre of their circle, where a single youth stood. "You think you're so high and mighty now, don't you? Just because you have the Jarls' blessings? We all know who you are. Princess Vírún picked you out of the mud and you pretend your stinking coat of shit is spun gold."

"Giving himself airs," another said. "Just because the princess enjoys being stuffed full of Viking cock."

"Don't you dare," snarled the youth. "Don't you *dare* speak of Princess Vírún in that way."

"Oh, go on," the Jomsviking laughed. "Go on, then. Keep on licking the Christian woman's cunt. It's served you well so far, hasn't it?"

A round of jeers, the threatening crackle of Vyrgen growls.

The youth unsheathed his seax in a hiss of metal.

The others all jeered and whooped at the suggestion of a fight. Chest tightening, I squinted at the youth in the darkness. He was standing in the middle of the crowd of men, hunched and ready. The starlight threw silver dust over his tousled blond hair, glittered on the bumps of his scar.

Thrain Mordsson.

"Oho! Let's do it, boy," the bearded Jomsviking said. "Who wants to fight Thrain Mordsson with me? I offer my sister's hand if we win."

"Your sister's an ugly wart," another shouted, drawing laughter. "But I'll fight with you!"

"Aye! And me," another stepped in.

Thrain Mordsson was alone against three. The others all spaced out in a circle to watch.

My hand tightened on the reins. As Jarl, I knew I should step in and prevent it. But I was so curious to see how this particular hero fought. Surely if he could best groups of Vyrgen as a boy, these three would pose no real threat to him.

"Looks like you're all alone, boy," the Jomsviking snarled with relish. "Do you want to call for Princess Vírún? So you can hide in her skirts some more?"

"You're talking a lot for a man who wants to die," Thrain snarled.

The Jomsviking only laughed. "It's far past time someone put you back in your place, *pup.*"

And then he lunged.

My breath stopped in my throat as steel met steel. The Jomsvikings were fighting with swords and axes – and Thrain met them at every angle, parried every attack. The moon was near gone and yet he was too fast to register, spinning to clash with their weapons, throwing them off with unnatural strength.

Blood spattered the ground in an arch. The three assailants paused, stepped back. Thrain's hair was in his face as he snarled at them, breathing the angry rasping breaths of a pup who has not yet learned to growl.

"Always fighting dirty," the Jomsviking growled. "You're getting slow, pup. Is that all you—"

Thrain's seax flew and *thunked* into the Jomsviking's neck.

A gurgling cry of pain broke the snowy silence. The man staggered back, hands on his neck, rejoining his fellows who closed ranks around him. And then they were on Thrain – four, five, six of them all at once.

Thrain slipped an axe from his belt and met them squarely. Envy pulsed through me as I watched him take them on without even hesitating. That boy had unnatural skill. He was younger than me and he fought like *that*, he'd developed that skill alone! It was like he had no fear…

... and then he turned, and I saw the expression on his face.

Pure fear. Pure fury. The whites of his eyes shone; his teeth were bared. He was fighting for his life, and while his movements were graceful and fluid, he had the air of a hunted animal.

That was not the face of a heroic wanderer. That was the face of pure desperation.

Three more Jomsvikings fell to Thrain's axe. He drew long shredded banners of blood through the air with it. Their corpses trailed intestines where they'd fallen. It was getting uglier – and when retaliation came for Thrain, he was cut and pummelled, receiving as rough a treatment as he gave.

I could see then that there was nothing glorious about his solitude. He was fighting without even calling for help. Perhaps he didn't believe it would come, as he had never had the privilege of help.

Of pack.

"*OY!*" I yelled, turning Alsvithr's head. They barely heard me – the ruckus they were making was waking all of Dublin. Karls and thralls alike were drifting out into the snow to see what the fuss was, pulling their shawls tighter over their shoulders.

I trotted up to the mess of men locked together in the brawl, shouting, "Down! *Stand down!*"

The Jomsvikings broke apart the melee, staggering away. As pack leader, I had nurtured the type of bark that commanded obeisance, even by men who were not my pack. These men were older and larger than me; it was always satisfying to be obeyed by their ilk.

But Thrain did not stay down for long. He saw opportunity in their stillness.

"Thrain—" I started, but he'd already lunged. His axe

sailed and the edge caught one of the men in the groin, spewing blood, making him yell in agony.

And chaos broke out again.

I jumped down from Alsvithr, unsheathed my sword. "Thrain Mordsson, you will STOP," I barked, and his body twitched, his face contorted with pain – but he ploughed through my intent, renewing his butchery until only four Jomsvikings were left out of the dozen who had attacked him.

Several watching Dubliners ran to arm themselves and join me. My blood sang in the heat of the improvised battle as they stood with me. They pulled back the Jomsvikings while I went to engage Thrain Mordsson.

I swallowed hard as I approached the furious pup. The very idea of fighting him sent a thrill up my spine, tightening my muscles.

I waited for him to swing again and dove in, sweeping my sword up to knock his axe off-target. His wide eyes turned to me. We held the position – his axe was curved around my blade, both of us locked there, feet planted wide apart.

I growled at him, fierce and loud, and he winced.

"Down, pup," I barked.

"This isn't your fight, Jarl," he said through a bloody mouth.

"You're on my turf," I said. "You will not spill your bad blood here."

"Oh? I thought you were enjoying the sights from over there."

"I thought it would only be a brawl," I snapped. "Not this wanton butchery! You are all here to serve Princess Vírún; Dublin is your home now as well as hers. I don't know what it's like up there in the Uí Néill, but here we don't shit where we eat."

He slid his axe around my blade, disengaging in a hiss of metal. But he did not stand down. To my surprise he only stepped back and resumed a defensive stance, eyes flickering between me and the pacified Jomsvikings behind me, who were being held by my Dubliners.

From Thrain's face, he did not differentiate between us. He saw only foes.

"Calm down," I urged him. "We are not your enemies, Thrain. Many of us are travellers too, far from our homes. Many of us are Vestfold men who've suffered the same as you. We're kin."

It was the wrong thing to say. A terrible smile lifted his mouth.

"Vestfold men," he hissed. "Vestfold men who stare and do nothing while blood is spilt in their streets. Vestfold men who drink themselves stupid and chase the Vanirdøtur or whatever other idiotic fantasy while our homeland burns. Yes, you are Vestfold men indeed. And I have no kinship with you."

I breathed out slowly, trying to gauge whether he would attack again. Though there was no red glow on account of the waning moon, there was so much anger in his face.

It made me wonder what he was like in his moon-craze, if this was him on a regular night.

I raised my voice, restating my authority. "So what do you plan on doing for the homeland? Are you going to ride out all by yourself?" I tried to ignore the pang of familiarity as I said the words. It pained me, how much of myself I recognised in him. "A solitary Varg does not amount to much. The real idiot is the one who believes he does not need pack."

And that made both of us idiots, standing in the snow, refusing the idea of dependency on other people.

Thrain's mouth opened, but he hesitated on his answer. In the silence I quoted Odin's Hávamál, for both of our benefits:

> "On the hillside drear, the fir-tree dies,
> stripped of its needles and bark;
> it is like a man whom no one loves.
> Why should his life be long?"

Thrain lifted his chin, surprised that I would bring poetry to this bloodbath. Then, wearing a defiant expression, he quoted back to me:

> "A witless man, when he meets with men,
> had best abide in silence."

I grinned despite the insult. So he knew his Hávamál. Then again, he was the son of a Jarl; it should not have surprised me.

"I'm here for the princess's sake," Thrain spat. "Once she has no more use of me, I don't plan on staying. I don't need your sorry excuse for a pack, nor your shithole of a settlement."

My smile flattened again. Now that — *that* I would not abide. I stepped forward, raising my sword; he responded instantly, raising his left-handed guard.

"I suppose you think insulting us makes you sound like a man?" I growled at him. "On the contrary. It's below you. You're the most notorious Norseman on this island — you've killed kings, you have a name that sits on the tongue like the fingertip of a god. And yet all I see is a frightened pup who's wasting his own potential."

He dipped his chin, eyes meeting mine with that feral eagerness for blood.

"You think I'm afraid?" he snarled.

"Yes," I breathed. "I can recognise it. You aren't the only one who's suffered, Thrain."

He swiped at me, not letting me speak another word. I drew my sword, breathing hard as I parried with a *clang*. His left-handed attacks left me scrambling; I had to strain at odd angles to better take his attacks. He had me backing away as I scarpered from his jabs, picking up my feet when he went for my shins.

Crafty little fucker. He was fast and vicious.

But so was I.

We disarmed one another at the same time, a screech of steel ending in both weapons flying from our grasps. I caught him, kneed him hard in the stomach. But he pulled me down with him, arm locked around me, both of us pitting our full body weight against one another.

The Dubliners around us had given us a wide berth. Some were cheering. I could hear them calling to one another – *come and see! It's Ivar, Ivar's fighting Thrain Mordsson!*

The idiots didn't seem to think I might be having a tiny bit of trouble against this *notorious regicide*.

Thrain had me on the floor in moments. He straddled me, holding my wrists over my head. Pain, sharp and vivid, speared across my torso – my wound had cracked open again. I hadn't felt it at first, but now that I was stretched across the floor the stitches were opening wider.

Indignity twisted through my guts. Nobody had held me down like this in a long time. I gritted my teeth, glaring up at him, noting that my Dubliners were all watching in rapt silence now. The sweetness of Thrain's scent took the edge off my anger; he smelled of mulled wine and the snowy cold that cloaked us both.

"What are you going to do now?" I hissed. "Kill the men who would offer you friendship?"

"I'm thinking about it," Thrain snarled.

"And then?" I said. "Where will you go, once you've washed your hands of Dublin? What is it that you hope to accomplish?"

His grip on my wrists tightened, his eyes wild. "I will go to Vestfold," he said, and his words were imbued with righteous rage, a ringing depth, like listening to a Völva invoke the gods. "I will tear out Harald Fairhair's heart. Then I'll find his family and make sure there isn't a single man left alive that can carry his name."

Goosebumps pricked my skin as I held that murderous gaze. "And if he kills you?"

"Then we will go to Valhöll together, and I will kill him there, over and over again," he hissed, almost manic now, his eyes gleaming with the pleasure of his fantasy. "Until Fenrir devours us all, and I can be content."

He was mad. He didn't care if he destroyed himself.

Admiration thrummed in my chest as I held the boy's gaze. He was absolutely feral, just as Vírún had said. But I wholly recognised his lust for the great direwolf's teeth, the end of all things. How it would sweep away all of our problems. It was an image I basked in too, sometimes, when the world threatened to overwhelm me.

"I can well imagine it," I muttered. "Whether in Vestfold or Valhöll. You would be magnificent."

The madness in him made way for mute confusion. He had not expected flattery nor admiration.

"You can accomplish your vengeance," I said. "I know you can. I can see it. But you don't have to destroy yourself in the process. A pack would give you solid foundations. A pack would save you, give you a place to return to at day's end."

Just like my pack had saved my own arse, time and time again, when I pursued my own self-destructive paths.

Thrain's eyes flickered between mine, still speechless with surprise. Under his feverish fury, I wondered if he could feel that yearn for kinship arise from where he'd buried it.

"Don't you want that?" I added softly.

There were shadows in the corners of my eye, feathery footsteps in the snow. Thrain twitched, made to look over his shoulder – but an axe found his throat before he could move very far.

The curve of the axe embraced his neck, forced him to straighten up. I could scent Olaf, feel his presence before I saw him looming behind Thrain.

"Down," he growled, voice low and dangerous, his gaze sweeping between us to ascertain who was wounded. When he saw the blood pooling over my waist, his eyes widened in fear. "What has he done? Are you all right?"

Olaf. My brother. My failsafe ally.

I had been gripped by my own bout of madness, to have thought of leaving him tonight.

"Let him go," I told my brother as I sat up, curling an arm around my waist. "The Jomsvikings attacked him. I got tangled in the fight. He didn't mean to harm me."

Thrain, caught upon Olaf's axe as he was, frowned down at me.

Several Dubliners rushed to help me up now that Olaf had Thrain in hand; they hauled me to my feet, pulling my arms around their shoulders.

"I count eight dead," Olaf muttered, glancing around at the carnage. It was damning enough to send Thrain packing if I did not take his side. "They really attacked you?"

"Yes. Thrain acted in self-defence," I said. "We should send the others back to the Uí Néill. We have no need of them here if they're going to bring violence to our doorstep." Then, meeting my brother's eyes, "Any friend of Vírún's is our friend, isn't that right? I don't think she needs any more guards when she has you and Thrain Mordsson."

Olaf's face went blank as he realised I had eavesdropped on their earlier conversation. No doubt he was going back over it, trying to guess what else I'd heard.

"We'll see about that," he said at long last. Then, to Thrain: "Are you going to stand down if I let you go?"

"Yes, Jarl," Thrain wheezed through the pressure of the axe.

Olaf slowly slid away the curved metal. Thrain remained kneeling; he placed his hands in the dirt, bowing his head to Olaf in apology and submission.

"I'm sorry," he said to the dirt, speaking through gritted teeth. He was frowning, coming down from the violence, the madness clearing from his mind.

"Get up," Olaf barked at him. His eyes were on my injury; he did not spare Thrain any pleasantries or accolades this time, worried as he was for me. "We have work to do to clean up this mess."

ᛁᚠᚾᚱᚱ

Olaf leaned over my bed, needlessly folding the covers over me. I'd been given milk of the poppy, enough to make my head spin, so there were lots of Olafs looking drawn and miserable on the edge of my bed.

"How do you feel?" he asked.

"Like Máni riding the clouds," I slurred, and he scoffed.

"Give it a few days and you should be able to walk."

"Mmmm."

He pointlessly smoothed out the covers again, working up the courage to speak.

"I'm sorry you overheard Vírún and I," he said. "Honestly, you shouldn't have been eavesdropping in the first place."

I coughed a laugh. "Difficult not to," I said. "I live here too, you know."

He'd been suspicious about why I'd been out at all last night, and why I'd taken Vírún's horse with me. Something told me he'd guessed my intent to run into the night, to hurt him right back. To lift my chin like an angry child and say, *I can do just fine without you.*

We had not spoken of it outright. But it hung between us, assumptions and bitterness. Such it was, between Olaf and I – words weren't often needed to let accusations be felt.

He patted the covers in search of my hand, grasped it in his large bear's grip.

"I said things about you that I didn't mean," he said quietly. "I was angry that you'd be so dismissive of Vírún, when she makes so much effort to please us."

"I know," I muttered. "You're well suited, both of you. She's a fine woman."

Olaf's mouth twitched into a private smile. "She is."

"You know… those things you said," I went on. "You made it sound like I'm content to drift and dream. But in reality… I'm not."

"I spoke in frustration. You do far more than drift and dream—"

"You and I both know the accusation isn't unfounded," I insisted.

Laced with the poppy milk, the humiliation of having

lost to a pup was making all of my bitterness bubble out of me. Olaf's hand tightened around mine as he waited for me to elaborate.

"I've always wanted to be more like you," I admitted to him. "You're so damned sure of yourself. Whatever legacy you want – you simply reach out and take it."

Olaf scoffed. "You make it sound easy."

"You make it *look* easy," I countered.

"You've always had impossibly high standards," Olaf said with a smirk. "You know you could have anything you want, if you simply put your mind to it and accept what comes to you."

"*Anything*... is that right?" I smiled as the concept danced in front of me. "Ah, brother... but you know how it is. A bastard dare not dream so high."

"You're an idiot if you believe that," Olaf said. "What were you going to do, when you did come face to face with a Vanirdottir? Excuse yourself and say you couldn't be with her, because *a bastard dare not dream so high*?"

I scoffed. "Probably." Then, meeting his eye: "Interesting that you said *when*, not *if*."

"I told you, I'm not abandoning the chase." He squeezed my hand again. "I know what it means to you, little brother. I wouldn't deny it to you. Especially not if it means you'll hare off into the wilderness and keep at it alone."

"I was being stupid," I admitted. "I thought I was losing you to all of this. To Vírún."

"That is stupid," he rumbled.

"I *am* losing you a little," I said. "You'll be a husband come the full moon. And a father, soon after that."

"Now don't try and go too fast like that," Olaf said through a smile. "I still plan on enjoying my courtship."

I paused, breathing softly. The drugged tiredness was making me open up until I was raw and naked, like the wound in my side. "Truth is," I said, "when I saw Thrain all alone like that... I realised it was pointless to go and pursue the hunt myself. Fulfilling this dream will count for naught if I can't share it with you."

He let out a *tch* as he stared down at me, his expression going all soft. Then, composure cracking to reveal the big sentimental bear that he was, he could not resist leaning over me for a hug.

"I never wanted you to leave," he grumbled.

I grabbed his shoulders, holding him tighter. "I didn't really want to, either."

"Good. Try it again and I'll drag you back by the ear."

I laughed, the poppy milk turning it to weak shudders. Olaf let me go, settled me back into the pillows and pressed his hand on my shoulder.

"Get some rest. I need you fit enough to dance at my wedding."

Chapter 6

I took my place in the groom's mats, angling my tagelharpa upon my lap. My bow slid down the strings, drawing a liquid sound, like sliding a finger along the surface of a still lake.

The moon was high; the Irish guests all gone. It had been a beautiful ceremony, if a little chaotic. Vírún wore a green gown that wholly flattered her, and she'd smiled when I offered to dance with her.

We had reconciled over the weeks, slowly but surely. I deferred to her, included her in conversation, showed her all the due respects. We did not have much in common other than Olaf; I couldn't quite navigate her brand of excessive formality, the façade of calm composure she wore around us. But I couched respect in all my gestures, and she appreciated the efforts I made nonetheless. Our greatest victory was to share comfortable silences together; an important thing, when she was to live with us.

We had done away with her Jomsvikings. She had not protested much at all; she considered Thrain as a little brother of sorts, and she agreed that it posed an unnecessary risk to force them to cohabitate. She didn't really need any more guardians than one as lethal as Thrain, anyway. That, and we knew she wanted him and his mother to flourish here alongside her, under her watchful eye.

Vírún had kept Thrain close throughout the daylight ceremony, but he had retreated as soon as the moon rose. He was still young; I had to wonder how he spent his full moons, if he attended feasts yet. Perhaps he still worked through the night as Vyrgen adolescents are made to do.

Of course, the Dubliners weren't going to leave him on the outskirts of this feast. They were all far too enthusiastic at the idea of having Thrain Mordsson in our midst. The fact that he had beaten me in a duel only endeared him to them; they found his strength so admirable that they forgave him for his irascible nature.

We'd arranged the courtyard of the great hall so that furs and benches surrounded the central fire pit, stars blinking overhead. There was dancing, still, but couples and groups were beginning to form. Thrain was perched on a bench, looking anywhere but at the lustful couples. Someone had forced a horn of mead in his hand, which he sipped from grudgingly.

Olaf and Vírún were near the fire, surrounded by flower offerings, half-naked in the furs. I had positioned myself to give them privacy; Vírún had agreed to this because she wanted to adhere to our customs, but I knew she was uncomfortable exposing herself like this.

Every now and then I glimpsed her face through the flames as they moved together. She was wearing a frown, her face sweaty, her hair loose so she could hide in it. Olaf would slick it back over her head, lean their foreheads together, patiently letting her set the pace though the rut was upon him.

She was being brave for him.

Mostly, I let my eyes rest on Thrain as I slid my bow over the strings of my tagelharpa. We had not talked at all in the past weeks; he had been as elusive and silent as ever. But there was something thoughtful about him, something calmer ever since the other Jomsvikings had been dismissed. Even now, from time to time, he would stare into thin air as I drew my songs around us, as though listening intently and trying to pretend he wasn't.

It was very difficult to ignore him. *Beautiful* was still how I'd describe the young man. He would be handsome in a few years, perhaps; when that dagger-sharp jawline had earned more of a beard, when he lost the youthful smoothness of his skin.

For now… he was attracting quite a few pairs of eyes. I could feel a possessive growl building, the urge to fend them off shivering behind my teeth.

He was still a little shit. A reckless little arsehole who'd fought me *and won* on my own territory. We had a rematch due, especially now that my wound was fully healed.

That meant he was *mine*.

With the moon silvering my blood, I tried as best I could to stay concentrated on my playing, my fingers moving with more and more of a tremor. It did not help when Thrain's eyes wandered, watching my hands, the moon giving his gaze a fixed, mesmerised quality.

Men were coming together in the furs and on the outskirts of the feast. I couldn't resist slipping into a familiar song, a piece of Odin's Hávamál that was an ode to fraternity. The syllables stretched out, making it a long, languorous song that let no one misinterpret its true meaning:

> "Young was I once, and wandered alone,
> And naught of the road I knew;
> Rich did I feel when a comrade I found,
> For man is man's delight."

Thrain's icy blue gaze flickered up to meet mine as the last syllable left my tongue.

Then the moment came, distracting us. Many heads turned as Olaf and Vírún moved, readying for the claiming. She lay beneath him; he waited for her to be ready, his heavy-lidded eyes gauging her expression. There was a red glint there; his moon-craze was close. As ever his self-control was admirable as he moved with slow grace over his wife, readying to knot her.

She was breathing hard, frowning, hair stuck to her face with sweat. There was fear in her scent, in the way she gripped his shoulders, fingers clenching and unclenching rhythmically.

He was careful, but the more he advanced, the deeper her frown became. When he stopped and retreated, she gave a whimper of relief. There was enough noise and merriment around to drown their voices, but a focused ear could still pick them up.

"It's all right," Vírún whispered. "It doesn't... doesn't hurt."

Her whole body was so tense, I could see it from where I sat, from what little I glimpsed between the flames.

"Please," she sighed. She was close to tears. "I promise I'm fine..."

"Hush. You aren't ready. We have time."

He leaned in to kiss her neck, returning to more

shallow movements, and she clung to him as they sank back into more familiar pleasures. I could taste salt on the air, her tears mingling with the sweat of many revellers.

"I want to please you," she whispered, her voice thick with sorrow.

"You do please me, Vírún," Olaf rumbled. "You please me very much. I can only hope I please you just the same."

She gave a strangled little noise, then pulled him in to kiss him. There was gratitude there; a desperate gratitude to be judged worthy by a man like him.

I recognised it all too well. That striving to be good enough, though it meant wading through pain. Perhaps she and I had more in common than I had suspected.

Thrain was wearing a peculiar expression as he watched them. The hand wrapped around his horn of mead was holding it so hard I expected it to fly into shards. There was an intensity in his gaze, but I couldn't quite tell whether it was anger or arousal or something else.

When they finally managed the knotting, Vírún threw back her head as Olaf held her firm against him, her mouth open around a shuddering breath.

"Hurts," she gasped. "It hurts—"

Empathy stung me upon hearing her words. It was too late now to retreat again; it would only hurt her more.

"Give it time," Olaf growled, his voice rocky and deep. "You have to let go. Let yourself go."

His teeth were growing; it was a good thing she was facing away from him, so she wouldn't see how the moon-craze was spilling red madness over his eyes. He rocked inside her, rutting her slowly so she might relax and accommodate him.

It took time; it always did. Thrain had dipped his chin,

glaring at them now. He was not happy to hear Vírún's pain, that much was obvious. But surely he knew there was nothing to be done.

Olaf managed to hold back from biting her until the tensions had smoothed, until the breaths that left her were pleasure rather than pain. But his eyes were spitting red by then, almost completely gone – his mouth hovered by her neck, teeth against her skin, letting her prepare for what was coming. Then finally he had to give in, to let it overtake him.

She cried out as he sank his teeth into her neck. Thrain stood, outrage brimming from him. The others that loitered around him reached for him, calling for him to calm down. But he broke from their grasps, starting toward the fire.

I put aside my tagelharpa and stood. Thrain's eyes were growing red; he was letting his anger get the better of him.

I strode across the fur-strewn floor where many revellers were indulging themselves. He couldn't rip his eyes from his mistress, even as I stood right in his face and gripped him by the tunic.

"Stand down," I commanded, growl rumbling in my chest. "Oy. Look at me."

He finally obeyed. His eyes were rimmed with red, his scent spiking deliciously as he let his rut take over. I marched him back to the benches, my growl working to push back his instincts.

I could not help the thrill of arousal that coursed through me as I sat my dominance over him. That he might defer to me was natural – of course he should, he was young and I was pack leader, it was the order of things. But there was still pride in overcoming this particular young man.

"He's hurting her," he huffed, his voice warped and scratchy.

"The biting always hurts. She'll do it to him, when she's ready," I told him. Then, with a grin; "This is your first full moon feast, isn't it?"

He started, every bit the pup caught doing something he shouldn't. "No," he lied.

"Sit down," I barked. He obeyed, reflexively moving his head to the side. With the rut upon us, his instincts were far more on the surface, responsive now where before he had keenly resisted me.

I sat beside him. He needed supervising, and my rut would not allow any other Varg to try and tame this one. There was some form of grudging respect between us; it was flattering, that he would recognise my pull as pack leader, though he was not officially part of the Dublin pack yet.

Olaf also trusted me to keep everyone relatively civilised while Vírún was still among us. It was my duty.

Vírún and Olaf had collapsed onto their sides; she was recovering, fingers digging into the furs, panting. He loomed over her, nuzzling her hair. His eyes were still fully red, his teeth sharp as ever – while she had not bitten him back, he would remain feral. But he was a gentle beast while he was knotted to her; he stayed in the crook of her neck, scenting her, reassuring her with the deep rumble of his growl.

The mood was growing heady as many others consummated their lust around us, or watched while drinking their fill. Vírún moved with a groan of effort, and with some careful manoeuvring, they managed to shift positions. Olaf lay beneath her while she sat perched upon him, shivering, pulling her half-undone dress closer around herself.

It was time for her to mark him back. She held her metal canines in her shaking grip. Olaf stroked her thighs, waiting, watching her as she brought the device to her mouth and hesitated. She seemed a little frightened as she looked into Olaf's pure red eyes.

"I don't want to hurt you," she muttered.

"Come," he growled, his voice distorted and deep as Odin's himself. "Come here."

Bravely she tucked the device into her mouth. Then she leaned over him – and I watched, mute with awe, as my brother bared his neck for her.

He did not bare his neck for anyone. Perhaps Father, when they had their disagreements and tempers flared, but that was the only authority Olaf recognised.

She bit into him, her loose black hair fanning over her back. He held her closer, claws digging into her – "Harder," he growled, and it took a little longer before she pierced him properly. And he squeezed his eyes shut, letting out a groan that was more animal than man, caging her against his huge body.

A cheer rose from the environing revellers, ululations rising into the night sky. Vírún was shaking when she pulled away from her husband, dropping her bloody canines to her hand. Surely it was the imminent escape from the depravity of this feast that moved her to act. Olaf, restored to himself at last, bore them through the gentle aftermath of the rutting before bundling her up in his arms and rising to leave.

I held my horn up for them, initiating the toast; many more lifted goblets and cups in celebration.

"Congratulations," I said, keen to fulfil my role, though that familiar hollow feeling was tugging at my chest as they stole away together. "Enjoy the moon."

Olaf nodded at me, looking haggard and not altogether

restored to sanity. He'd monumentally held back tonight. I wondered if he realised he had dedicated himself to restraint, since his appetites were so large and his wife so clearly delicate.

"Enjoy the moon, all of you," he grunted over his shoulder. "Don't give my brother too hard a time."

Jeers rose at that, and I grinned, saying, "Nothing I can't handle."

Chapter 7

With Vírún gone, the musicians took up wilder tunes, the drums beating faster. Everyone was growing feverish with the moon at its pinnacle; without the Christian princess to behave for, they let out keenings and cries, groups pulling together so that many bodies twined in shared lust.

Thrain rose, his body slanted, his face shining with sweat. His breathing was laborious now, his rut fully overtaken him. I bumped his shoulder, held him there a moment as I scanned the courtyard, making sure no one was getting too chaotic.

"Going somewhere?" I asked him.

"Leaving," he grunted.

I grinned. "No you're not."

There was something furtive about the way he looked at me. I could scent the arousal on him, the pulse of hot blood.

"I'm keeping an eye on everyone tonight," I said. "Making sure it stays civilised."

"If I stay," he said haltingly, "it won't be civilised."

"You realise how that sounds to me," I said softly. "If you haven't learnt control, you need someone to help you."

"No."

The answer was reflexive, spat from between lips that were lined with sweat.

"What's the alternative?" I said. "You'll go and chop wood all night? Drink all our reserves? Go hunting alone?"

He let out a scoff. "What I do is my business."

"It's *my* business, to maintain control over my Vyrgen under the full moon," I muttered. "You're here. You're one of mine now. You need to learn control."

"I'm not one of yours," he snarled. "I don't trust you."

"I don't trust you, either," I snapped back. "You're old enough to break. I want to keep my Dubliners safe from any eventuality."

He scoffed, as though insulted that I might imply he was unsafe for the men and women here.

"You can't stop me leaving," he quipped. "You could barely handle me under the waning moon. For a pack leader, you're pretty pathetic."

I raised my eyebrows, the clear challenge sparking heat at the base of my spine.

"You really are a little shit," I said on a grin. He made to move past me, butting his shoulder into mine. I caught him, making two fists in his tunic, holding him close enough to butt heads. "You're staying right here."

"Make me," he hissed.

My grin widened. "All right."

He moved – faster than ever, eeling under my grasp.

I caught him by the belt, relishing the moon's influence, how my stretching muscles sang. We grasped at one another, feet spaced out on the ground, each trying to catch the other's wrists.

I hit first, drawing a line of blood from his mouth. When he turned back to me, his eyes were ringed red, that bloody line trickling down his chin. His hair was all in his face again, sharp blond strands touching his lips.

Loki. He shouldn't have been so damned attractive. The sight and smell of him had me growling like I was the one with impulse control issues.

"*Braaawwl!*" came a spirited shout. There were eyes on us, men slamming their goblets against the benches, chanting: "Rematch! Rematch!"

"Get him this time, Ivar!"

Thrain was on me like a starved wolf. I barely had the time to anticipate his movements before he'd dragged me down into the furs, his shoulder crashing against my stomach, knocking the air from my lungs.

We struggled. Letting out the full force of my growl worked to my advantage – he would weaken his grip despite himself, and I'd pull him down under me, holding him there by a twist of the arm or a fist in his hair.

He needed someone to temper him. Someone more mature, to tame his wild edges. But he was a dangerous young man; and I had some wild edges of my own.

Still. I wanted to rise to the task. To hold all of his raw power under me, pinned between my thighs – it was intoxicating.

To think I could claim dominance over someone like him.

He was livid that his instincts might work against him. He fought them as hard as he could, so that every twitch of instinctive submission was a hard-won victory.

Then, at long last, out of sheer frustration — a potent growl broke out of his throat, rumbling deep and rich.

He intended it to be intimidating. But it was the most arousing thing I'd ever heard; especially as it was completely uncontrolled.

He noted my surprise. Grabbed me by the waist, and *slammed* me to the dirt.

I coughed as the dirt cloud rushed into my lungs. He pinned me down, displacing the fur pelts even more, scattered and messy as they were from our brawl.

I gazed up at him, heart racing deliciously. My instincts roared that this fucking pup might be holding my wrists above my head *again*. There was a dangerous sheen of crimson in his eyes, taking over now.

He was diving deep into his moon-craze.

And I couldn't wait. Just to see what he'd do. What he was capable of.

It shouldn't have been so erotic — but Freya, his potent rage weakened me entirely.

He was panting, breath hot against my mouth, his sweat dripping down onto me. I twisted in his grip; he was straddling me, crushing the hard length of my cock.

I bucked up against him and found him just as hard as I was.

Oh.

That was… interesting. And wholly too flattering.

He frowned, eyes fluttering shut as I pressed up against his thigh, crushing the rigid length that was trapped under his breeches.

"Better, isn't it?" I hissed. "Having the right company."

"Shut up," he growled, and *gods*, that rumbling thunder in his chest was pummelling me in all the right places.

"I know this is difficult for you," I taunted. "But it doesn't have to be."

"Shut *up*," he insisted, his voice barely recognisable, wrapped as it was in his growl.

He could've left. He had completely incapacitated me. But he stayed.

"Is there something you want to say to me, pup?" I taunted, pressing up against that ridge again, feeling him pulse with excitement.

His eyes... gods, this was getting dangerous.

He leaned in and bit my neck, *hard*. I gasped at the sheer outrage of it — he was biting *me* — him, claiming blatant dominance over me on my own territory!

But that wasn't all that bite meant.

I laughed as he ground his teeth into me, his tongue flattened hungrily against my skin.

Thrain Mordsson... wanted *me*. Gods, I could get used to this type of flattery.

"Well, if that's what you wanted," I purred, arching up into his grip, "why didn't you just say so?"

He bit harder. I could hear a faint whine in his throat, the neediness of it travelling straight down to my erection.

He was unravelling.

I lifted my head, bit him back hard in the neck, tasting the salt on his skin. He winced, let go, twitched his head. Turned just a little to give me ease of access.

Loki, his body was so responsive to me. He wanted me to touch him; he was testing me, testing to see whether I was worthy enough for him to relinquish control.

He was aching to submit. Give in to the craze, knowing someone could guide him safely through it.

The chink in his dominance was all I needed to topple him over. A push and shove and we'd rolled in the dirt, our roles reversed. I straddled him now, pinning his wrists in the dust.

Fear flashed across those corrupted eyes. I leaned

close, my growl turning to sweet reassurance, a caress I laid upon him. I gave him time, let him settle; he writhed and arched beneath me, barely conscious, a creature of pure instinct now.

Beautiful.

"Yield," I murmured as I watched him. "You're safe with me."

His growl was rising and falling, nervousness rippling through his body. I leaned over, bit into his neck again, catching the roped muscle properly this time and *squeezing*. He gave a delicious moan, turning his head for me, hips bucking up – and before long, a tremor ran along his body, his wrists twisting in my grasp as his breaths came fast and wounded in my ear.

I could smell it on him. Bitter musk trapped in sweaty leather. I'd made him come just like this.

Gods, he was a complete novice. First feast, indeed. I had to wonder if this wasn't the first full moon he'd spent in friendly company, since he'd begun developing the needs that came with maturity.

Had anyone ever even kissed him? Had he let anyone that close?

I lifted my head from his neck. To my delight, he kept his head turned, the perfect picture of submission, his eyes firmly shut as he rode the last waves of climax. I watched that open mouth, the shining curves of his lips.

Perhaps it would be pushing it.

Then again, he was rubbing his spent cock against me through his breeches, the scent of his climax twisting along my nerves, making my erection pulse.

I leaned in. He reacted instantly, glaring at me with those red eyes as our lips hovered close enough to taste. His growl rose, and I flattened it with mine, instincts glorying in his subjugation.

"That's it," I whispered, tracing the words against his lips. "Feels good, doesn't it? You don't have to fight it."

He was the one who bit me, sank his teeth into my lower lip. I responded; we were not engaging in something romantic, but rather devouring one another, snapping and snarling, tasting blood. I slowed him down, locked my tongue around his, gentle and crushing. Finally he calmed enough to follow where I lead. He was tentative, surprised, as though he had not expected gentleness could exist between two Vyrgen men.

Gods, he tasted so good. He had already had some relief; but he was working me up at an alarming rate.

I relinquished one hand from his wrists, wandered down his body. He tensed as I worked the laces of his breeches. I found him sloppy with his own cum, rigid as ever, his cock hot and slippery in my hand.

"Look at you," I whispered. "You're aching for someone to touch you, aren't you?"

He frowned, still unwilling to admit it, tangled as he was in pride and mistrust. But when I closed my hand around his cock, he threw back his head, eyes shut in delight. I grinned as I pumped him up and down, slow and firm, his hot girth so satisfying against my palm.

It didn't take very much longer. He was so hypersensitive; he bit his lip, pulsing against my fingers, trying to hold back.

"Don't fight it," I whispered. "You need this. You need to come; I can feel it. So come... be a good boy and come for me."

He whined, and when a hot stream erupted over my fingers, I smiled and purred, "Good boy... that's a good boy."

"Don't," he breathed, "you fucking – dare – call me that—"

I laughed. He'd pulsed and shivered at the words; it was clear he loved it.

"But you are," I murmured. "I know the first night isn't easy. It takes no small measure of courage to do this."

He frowned, breathing hard.

"We can stop if you prefer," I added. "I can lull you to sleep."

He met my gaze, his aggression turned now to tentative trust.

"No," he rasped. The words struggled past his pride: "Don't... stop."

Elation rose in me. He found me worthy.

I chanced going up a notch, freeing my cock from my breeches so that I could give us both some relief. He groaned as my smooth length slid against his, a velvety contact that had us shivering. I held us both in one hand, spreading his cum over us as I stroked up and down.

To have him spill his hot sticky cum at the same time as me – to catch us both in my hand, slipping and sliding over the mess we made – it made me feverish with desire. I needed... needed to hold him down and have him submit to me, willingly, completely.

Keeping his wrists firmly pinned down in the dirt, my free hand slipped between his thighs. This – this was another boundary. He glared at me, and I could see that fear returning. He had seen this; the orgy all around us offered a plentiful learning experience.

I pressed against his puckered entrance. My fingers were slippery and coated with both of our remnants; it would make an easy entry. His growl rose like a black crested wave, fear and indignation battering me.

"Trust me," I purred. "Once you know how this feels... you'll be begging me for it."

"I don't beg," he snarled.

Oh, you will, I wanted to tell him. But this trust between us was still a rickety thing; I would let his own body convince him that what I offered was pure pleasure.

I glided into him, stretching him. He was tense as a bowstring at first, body arching, thighs quivering around the intrusion. But I found that nook easily enough, his prostate already bulging against my fingertips.

Really, he was so easy.

I had him panting and whimpering in moments, the unfamiliar sensations rippling through his body, making him twitch and arch into me. I gorged myself on the sight of him, stretched out under me, completely vulnerable.

Completely giving himself up to me.

His cock was bulging as it lay against his stomach, rosy and leaking, inviting a mouth to clean it up. His impressive knot shone at the base, pulsing in time with his heartbeat. From the way he twisted his wrists in my grasp, I could tell he wanted to relieve himself.

"What is it, pup?" I asked him, grinning. "Is there something you want?"

He was too incoherent to reply.

"You want to touch yourself… could that be it?" I leaned closer just to taunt him. "I'd love to see it… what you look like when you stroke that gorgeous cock. Bet it'd feel good, wouldn't it?"

Red glinted in his eye as he glared at me. He knew exactly what I was doing.

"Well?" I said.

"Fuck you," he snarled.

"Suit yourself."

I *crushed* his prostate, massaging it so that he squeezed his eyes shut and quivered with ecstasy.

"You're… a fucking… arsehole," he hissed, making me grin.

"I'm really quite a nice man," I countered. "You just have to use the right words."

When he stayed resolutely silent, I dug my fingertips around the veiny bulge of his prostate, feeling it harden all the more as I toyed with him.

"Fine," I murmured. "Then I'll make you come like this."

His thighs were trembling by the time I had coaxed his prostate to the brink of orgasm; it was difficult for him, clearly, to reach climax without stimulating his cock at the same time. I took in his sweaty, panting state, curls of blond hair sticking to his cheeks... then gazed down at that pulsing cock, how absolutely inviting it was.

Fuck. He was glorious.

I laid a warning growl over him, making him twitch in surprise.

"Stay," I snarled. "If you can be good for me... I'll reward you."

I let go of his wrists and ventured down his body. He stared, keeping still, obeying for once. I glanced up at him, those beautiful corrupted eyes of his, and smiled as I hovered over his cock.

"Good boy."

With no further preamble, I sucked him deep into my throat. He chucked his head back, spine rising into an arch of pure abandon. I felt the pulses of his climax against my fingertips – his cum burst over my tongue, down my throat, thick and salty and delicious.

"*Fffffffuck,*" he groaned, and then he was invoking gods and swearing up and down the pantheon, making no sense whatsoever. His hands were in my hair, holding onto my braid as though to dear life.

It was... *copious*. I swallowed it down, bearing him through his climax, my own erection aching for even just a gust of fucking wind at this point, *anything* to relieve the yearn. Then when he was basking in the afterglow, I gave in to my own rut, turning him over roughly so that he lay on his front in the dirt.

He resisted, but he was limp in the aftermath of his climax. I shoved him down, forearm against his shoulder blades, growling my dominance. His arse was offered to me in this position, and the blatant submission of it had him tensing, broad back muscles shifting under my grasp as he tried to fight me off.

For all of his instinctive resistance, his thighs were already parted; he was panting against the earth, fingers digging into it. I stroked down the line of his back, along his nape and into his tousled hair, reassuring him.

"Settle," I soothed as he hummed and groaned, senselessly torn between the deep sexual urges of the rut and the Varg instinct for control. "Settle… that's it."

He reached down to take himself in hand as I bent over him, dragging my mouth along his shoulder. I let him feel my body heat all around him, my knees planted between his, my cock against the back of his thigh.

Taken over. Vulnerable. It took him a moment to acclimatise to the position, to hold until I could be certain he wouldn't throw me off.

"Good," I praised, straightening so I could glory in the sight of him on all fours in front of me. He backed up against my groin as though protesting that I might break the contact. Smiling groggily, I slid a hand down his waist. "Perfect. You've done so well, pup."

He sighed, wilting a little as he went on pulling at his cock. Oh, he loved the praise more than anything, I could tell as much.

When he came I caught his spend, lathered my cock with it, coating myself in the pearly white sheen. Then, biting my lip, I rubbed myself between his cheeks, shivering as my touch-starved cock got a sudden overload of sweet, slick slide.

His back dipped when I pushed into him. He was needier than ever, growling and whining under me, so deep in his rut now that he was blind to any attention we were garnering.

I pushed more and more still, stuffing him full of my cock, watching as it disappeared inside him. And he was lost in the intensity of it, bristling under me, undecided between backing up or moving away.

I grasped his hips and decided the direction for him.

Fucking a feral newcomer was always a little wild. But this being Thrain, a pup who could overcome me if he set his mind to it — it meant that I couldn't afford to be gentle nor distracted. He demanded everything that I had, every ounce of self-control, every last breath of stamina as he clawed at me, torn between mindless pleasure and the urge to take over.

I bit him to the blood, gave him the type of punishing rhythm that had us both slick with sweat. The firelight shone along the curves of his lean musculature, showing the half-moons of teeth and claws, the rise and fall of his ribs when he panted in between climaxes.

As the moon descended, I found myself needing pauses when he did not. The young and unruly were like that — half in the craze all night long, going beyond the capacities of their bodies. He would only stop to drink when I ordered him to, when the afterglow dimmed the rut just enough for consciousness.

It was difficult to manage the rest of the feast with him hogging my attention. Usually I flitted between partners, satiating myself here and there but otherwise patrolling. Now I had to delegate those duties to the older Vyrgen, whose needs were less fiery. They only grinned and happily took the responsibility.

There was respect in their expressions, that I might've tamed one such as Thrain. Pride glowed in me just the same, but it was more than just the idea of taming the man.

He trusted me. When he offered me his back, turned his head for my bite – he was trusting me entirely. And I was labouring to show him, as the night wore on, that I was worthy of that trust.

At least, I hoped it was indeed trust that was blooming between us. If he was throwing caution and consciousness to the wind, then we would have to have words come the morning.

I asked him while he was pinned under me, head tilted back, mouth open around a sigh. "Do you trust me now, Thrain?"

He opened those heavy-lidded eyes. Blue encroached with red; drops of blood in a clear, sunlit pool.

"Why are you so fucking talkative," he sighed.

I scoffed. "It's just a question."

"If you really can't tell," he managed, wheezing a little; he did have a huge cock buried in him, after all; "then you're an idiot."

I grinned and obligingly spared him more questions.

Chapter 8

THE DAWN smelled of charred wood, clean winter frost, and the sweat and spend of all the sleeping revellers. They'd piled into the great hall, bundled up under thick furs and wools.

Thrain had passed out in the early hours. I'd hauled him into the warmth of the great hall, then helped the other relatively conscious men to haul the last stragglers inside. We would roll the heavier drunkards, laughing when some awoke with yelped protests.

I was the last man awake, sitting by Thrain in the great hall, watching over everyone. Usually Olaf and I took turns to be the last man standing; this time of course, it defaulted to me.

I didn't mind. I loved the quietness of the aftermath, after a night of incessant drum-drum-drumming and howling chaos. My eyes swept the hall, taking them in, these men and women who were my pack.

To think I had almost left them. This was home; it was the home we had all built for ourselves. All these people were a part of it. Every single one had contributed. For a moment, that quiet thought brought a smile to my lips.

Home. Not some enchanted story to escape into; a real, solid place, with wooden pillars to lean against and the warmth of many bodies chasing away the winter cold. They stank, yes, but they were my people.

Sleeplessness clearly made me sentimental. I stared down at Thrain, who was propped on his side, breathing open-mouthed as he dreamed. His hair was in his face again; I reached down, brushed the wayward strands from his eyes.

It warmed me to have him here. Tonight, he was part of us.

I ran my fingers absent-mindedly through his messy blond hair as I sat there, exhausted but content. After a time he tilted his head, as though inviting me to continue.

I'd not seen him so unselfconscious before. I kept threading through his hair until his eyes blinked open, still groggily appreciating the contact.

Then, as I expected, he woke properly.

His whole body tensed. He shrank back from me, scrambling up to a sitting position, the furs falling from his body. He immediately felt for his seax at his lower back, eyes locked on mine. Distress flashed as he realised he was naked and unarmed.

"Easy. Looking for this?" I said softly, tapping the pile I'd made of his clothes. His sheathed seax sat on top of it. He stared as I lifted the seax and offered it to him in a clear gesture of trust.

"Just sit for a while," I told him as he warily took his weapon. "You were in and out of the craze last night; you should take a moment to recover."

He turned away from me, his face drawn as he shook out his breeches and pulled them on. I watched him, crestfallen by his defensiveness. Was he just as prickly as ever, or did it imply something else?

"That *was* your first feast, wasn't it?" I asked him. I didn't know how else to phrase the question; *what's your damage? Have men taken advantage of you?*

"I've seen Vyrgen feasts before," he grumbled. "Never got involved."

From his tone, I guessed it was his usual dislike of people and nothing more sordid than that. I doubted anyone could even approach him with ill intent and survive the encounter.

"Well? Are you glad you stayed this time?" I asked.

He gave a mirthless scoff as he drew his belt roughly and buckled it. "It's not like you gave me a choice," he muttered.

"I would've gladly lulled you to sleep," I said, grinning. "You're the one who took it in a different direction."

After that of course, he went back to his stony silence.

"I know you've managed alone up till now," I told him. "But your crazes will only get more intense as you mature. Here, sit." I reached for a nearby pitcher, poured him a goblet of warm, flat cider and passed it to him. "Sit for a while."

He sat and took the cider, keeping a small distance from me. I could still taste him on my tongue, the salt of his sweat, the tang of his cum; but now he stared glumly at the feast, completely ignoring me, as though we hadn't been locked together in complicated intimacy all night long.

Stubborn ass.

"Most of them are here," I said, gesturing at the crowd. "The Dublin pack. You've seen us now, you've been with us for a few weeks. We might not all be particularly likeable, but we trust one another as pack does."

Thrain stared sullenly at the furry heaps of sleepers. His stony façade was slowly crumbling as he sat in the quiet with me, listening to the snores and shuffles and whispers of the pack.

For just a moment, I glimpsed the young man he was. Lonely. Afraid. Yearning for a family to make up for the one he'd lost.

"They all admire you," I told him. "You might have treated them like the shit on your shoe these past weeks, but if you asked for their friendship, I know they would give it. You could have a place here, Thrain."

It seemed as though he might give in, then. But eventually he shook his head. "I can't," he said. "This easy life of yours—"

I laughed. "Easy, he says."

He glared at me. "To have a place here would mean to earn it," he said. "And keep on earning it. I'm not interested in earning your consideration; I told you, I don't plan on staying here forever. I don't care for *friends*."

"Maybe not *friends,* as in multiple," I indulged him, offering a tentative smile. "Maybe just the one friend. To start with."

He gave that small deadpan laugh again. Then he drained the last of his cider, let the cup fall in the furs, and pushed himself to his feet.

"You and I are never going to be *friends,* Ivar Gofraidsson."

*

Read more about Ivar and his pack in the main saga!

BOOKS BY LYX ROBINSON

The Viking Omegaverse
Stolen by the Wolves (Book 1)
Taming the Wolves (Book 2)
A Meeting of Wolves (Book 2.5)
The Summer Siege (Book 3)
COMING SOON: The Lady of Dublin (Book 4)

AFTERWORD

Originally a fantasy/SF writer, I took a sharp left turn in 2020 and got lost in the omegaverse. This probably explains why my smut ends up being pretty plot-heavy, as you can tell by now if you've gotten this far! My writing process is mainly fuelled by cheese (all the cheese), my undying love for historical reenactment, and folk bands that I am currently obsessed with. Thanks so much for reading & come say hello on my social media!

Sign up to my newsletter to keep up with my projects & get bonus material:
https://www.subscribepage.com/lyxrobinsonnewsletter

I love to hear from readers! Feel free to shoot me an email at: lyxrobinsonauthor@gmail.com.

Made in the USA
Columbia, SC
05 July 2024